DARK CHRISTMAS
A BRATVA NEXT DOOR ROMANCE

K.C. CROWNE

Copyright © 2024 by K.C. Crowne

All rights reserved.

No part of this book may be reproduced in any form or by any electronic or mechanical means, including information storage and retrieval systems, without written permission from the author, except for the use of brief quotations in a book review.

DESCRIPTION

I thought my neighbor was just a grumpy recluse.
Turns out, he's the devil in an Armani suit.

It all started with a Christmas disaster.
My curvy boudoir photos landed on *his* doorstep.
Cue absolute panic…
And visions of him laughing at my plus-size curves.

But when I showed up to reclaim my photos…
He wasn't laughing.
He was ***waiting***.
Dark eyes filled with hunger.
And my photos gripped tightly in his hand.

One night.
That's all it took—reckless, sinful passion to unravel me.
But the next morning brought shocking truth:
He's not just a brooding stranger.
He's a former Bratva boss, with blood-stained secrets and enemies in every shadow.

The snow might be falling gently outside,
But inside, I've walked straight into a storm.

And as if that wasn't enough…
I'm carrying his baby.

Reader's Note: This is full-length standalone, Christmas, bratva next-door, age-gap, romance. No cheating. HEA guaranteed.

CHAPTER 1

AMELIA

Holy fucking sexy accountant.

I can't stop staring at the man who lives across the street. I've only caught fleeting glimpses of him disappearing into his house or slipping into his car.

I've been calling him the sexy accountant in my head ever since I first laid eyes on him, though I have zero clue as to what he actually does for a living.

He's usually so... private. Mysterious, even. But today, he's out in the open, stretching on his front steps like he doesn't have a care in the world.

And damn, what a show.

It's a chilly November morning in San Francisco, but he's dressed as if were a summer day. His shorts hug his muscular thighs and his tank top shows off his strong, powerful-looking biceps and shoulders. Short salt-and-pepper hair and a neatly trimmed beard accentuate his square face and chiseled jaw.

He gives off an air of intelligence, like someone who reads a lot and takes an interest in world events. But his eyes—dark and dangerous—tell me there's more going on beneath that sharp exterior.

And his smile—disarming, secretive, and guarded. He looks like he could wreck my day and then cheerfully ask how it went afterward.

I'm trying to be subtle but in truth I'm openly gawking at him through my bedroom window like a creep.

Oh, shit. He's looking right at me.

Just as I'm about to duck out of view, he slips on a pair of sunglasses and takes off running.

An incoming text snaps me back to reality, my little fantasy about Mr. Tall, Dark, and Hot-as-Sin shattered. It's from Claire, my ride-or-die since high school, the one who was there when everything went sideways after my parents died. We run a bakery in the city together, and we've got big plans.

Hey, can you pick up some vanilla extract on your way in? We're fresh out. Again.

I roll my eyes but can't help smiling. I quickly shoot back a reply.

Got it. I'll grab extra this time.

With that handled, I toss my phone on the bed and head for the shower. I definitely need to wash away all the dirty thoughts after the show I just witnessed.

I stand beneath the stream, letting it cascade over me, my mind drifting right back to him and the way his muscles flexed and shifted with every move, his lean, powerful body in perfectly controlled motion. I bite my lip, feeling heat pool low in my belly.

Before I know it, my hand's sliding down my stomach, fingers grazing the sensitive skin between my thighs. But just as things are about to get interesting, I remember that I don't have time to let my fantasies run wild.

Damn it. I've got to pick up vanilla extract for Claire and my peeping has caused me to be running behind. I pull my hand away from where it was headed, forcing myself to get back to the basic business of showering like a functioning human being.

Once I'm done, I step out and dry myself, then head straight for my closet. I dress quickly in black jeans, an old comfy band t-shirt, and Chuck Taylors and I'm ready to slay the day.

I grab my keys, coat, and beanie, and head out the door. The crisp November air is invigorating. From my porch in the Mission District, I can see the fog just starting to lift, giving everything that dreamy, slightly eerie glow.

Lining the street and creating an image that looks straight off a postcard are the quirky yet iconic pastel-painted houses with little flower boxes under the windows.

I head down the street. First stop: coffee. I don't even have to say a word when I walk in. The barista, Zoe, spots me before I enter and nods, already putting the finishing touches on my order.

"Mornin', Am! Your iced oat milk latte with a double shot's already ready!" she calls out, sliding the drink across the counter.

"Thanks, Zoe! Lifesaver, as usual." I flash her a grin and slip a couple of bucks in the tip jar before grabbing my caffeine fix.

Sipping my coffee, I head back down the street. I live three blocks from the bakery, and I love my little daily commute. It's the perfect walk, especially when the weather's on point like today.

I run into the local grocery store, grab two bulk-sized bottles of vanilla extract, and head on to work.

I turn the corner and spot our bakery—Sweet Talk. It's housed on the first floor of a renovated Victorian, pastel blue with iconic bay windows and a quaint little porch out front. The white and pink sign above the door is cute but professional, and the little chalkboard sign out front always has some sassy quote of the day.

Today's reads: "Gobble 'til you wobble." Classic Claire.

As I get closer, the smell of fresh pastries hits me like a warm hug—sugar, cinnamon, a hint of pumpkin spice. My mouth's already watering.

With a grin on my face, I open the door, ready to dive into the day.

CHAPTER 2

AMELIA

I step in just in time to catch the daily cuteness overload of Claire giving her husband, David, a kiss goodbye. He's in his gym clothes, heading out for his pre-work workout, and they're both grinning like lovesick teenagers.

"Don't lift too heavy, mister," Claire teases, giving him a playful tap on the chest.

David chuckles, wrapping an arm around her and leaning in for a quick kiss. "You just focus on continuing to grow our little man in there," he says, resting a hand on her huge bump.

Claire can't hide her smile. "If he's anything like you, he'll come out flexing, ready to bench-press his crib."

It's such a wholesome scene I could gag, though I'm genuinely happy for her, of course.

David catches me watching and waves. "Morning, Am! Try to keep this one out of trouble while I'm gone," he says, gesturing to Claire.

Claire giggles. "You know that's a full-time job."

I laugh, shaking my head. "Yeah, I don't get paid enough for that."

David kisses Claire one more time, shooting her a wink before heading out the door. She watches him leave, her smile lingering, and I can't help but feel a little pang of jealousy.

"Girl, you are so lucky," I say, tossing my stuff down behind the counter and grabbing my apron. "Seriously, where does one find a man like that? Asking for a friend."

Claire laughs, brushing her long brown hair out of her face.

We get right into our usual routine, sliding into the flow like clockwork. Claire always shows up early to start on the breads; meanwhile, I'm all about the pastries, making sure everything's ready to roll by the time we unlock the doors.

"Here's hoping today's as nuts as yesterday," I say, tying my apron. "I'm still not over how we nearly sold out of everything."

"Seriously," Claire agrees, punching down a ball of dough. "Feels like we can barely keep up. Honestly, though, your holiday marketing is killing it. People are coming in droves."

I grin, pulling the vanilla extract out of my bag and setting it on the counter. "The trick is to get 'em in the door. The taste of the goods is the real marketing. They'll be back for more, no question."

Claire laughs. "True. One bite of your caramel apple turnovers and people are done for."

"Exactly." I start setting up for the day's fall specials, getting out the goods I'd prepped the night before. "So, I was thinking we'd do some pumpkin spice croissants—light and flaky, but filled with that sweet, creamy pumpkin goodness. And maybe some pecan pie Danishes. Oh, and when it gets closer to Thanksgiving, I've got a cranberry-orange scone recipe that'll knock their socks off. We'll throw in maple-glazed donuts, too, because, well, obviously."

Claire hums approvingly. "You're an evil genius."

"Thank you, thank you. I try."

I head into the back, ready to get to work. I start by rolling out the dough for the croissants, dusting the counter with flour, and carefully folding in the butter layers. The repetitive motion is soothing, but my mind starts drifting back to my sexy neighbor.

The image of his legs, muscles flexing with every stride as he ran off this morning, keeps replaying in my head. Those thick, powerful thighs. My hands move slower on the dough as my thoughts go from inappropriate to downright naughty.

I imagine him here in the bakery. He lifts me up onto the counter, flour flying everywhere as his lips trail down my body. His strong hands grip my thighs, pushing them apart as he—

Snap out of it, Amelia.

I shake my head, trying to get my brain out of the gutter, but it's not easy when the man across the street is literally sex on legs.

A knock on the window pulls me out of my daydreams. I glance up and see Mrs. Anderson and her daughter, Cynthia, standing outside. They're regulars, usually here at the crack of dawn for their coffee and a couple of muffins. Mrs. Anderson's waving at me, looking like she's got something on her mind.

I check my watch, it's a little before opening, but she's got that look that says this is more than just an early breakfast run. I wipe my hands on my apron and gesture for them to head to the front door.

I crack the door open with a grin. "Wow, you must really need your caffeine and muffin fix this morning."

Mrs. Anderson barrels inside and pulls me into a tight hug. I stand there, totally caught off guard, my arms awkwardly sticking out.

"Uh... what's this about?" I ask, laughing as I pat her back.

She pulls away, beaming. "It's for that cake you and Claire made for Cynthia's wedding shower!" she gushes. "It was absolutely stunning. You girls outdid yourselves!"

Cynthia, her daughter, nods enthusiastically, her designer bag slung over her shoulder. "Seriously, Amelia, it was the talk of the shower. Everyone was obsessed. I had to remind people to stop taking pictures and to actually *eat* it."

"Well, I'm glad it was a hit," I say.

"Yes, in fact, it went over so well, we want you to make the wedding cake, too!"

"Wow, really?" I reply, both surprised and flattered.

"Yes, really. We want something truly spectacular," Mrs. Anderson says. Cynthia nods excitedly. "We're going all-out."

Internally, I'm throwing a full-blown party. Wedding cakes are no joke, and landing this one is huge. "I'm sure Claire will be on board," I say, keeping my voice calm despite my excitement. "But I'll talk it over with her once she's done in the office."

"Perfect! We can't wait to see what you come up with," Cynthia says as they grab a couple of scones from the display.

I ring them up, watching them head out with a wave before going to the office and telling Claire the good news.

CHAPTER 3

AMELIA

"We're low on eggs, we need more butter, and I've gotta call Tony later about the sugar order—he shorted us last time. Oh, and don't forget, we need to double-check the yeast inventory before the Thanksgiving rush hits."

Claire pops out of the office, rattling off supply info like she's running a board meeting rather than a bakery.

I blink at her. "How do you do that? You're like a human calculator."

She shrugs like it's no big deal, and that's when I notice she's lugging two huge bags of flour. My jaw drops, and I rush over, easing the bags out of her arms before she can even think about protesting.

"C, what the hell? You're about to pop and you're out here playing Hulk with these flour bags? You're lucky I don't call David and snitch."

She rolls her eyes but gives me a grateful smile. "I'm fine, I swear. But thanks, Mama Bear. I guess you do need to keep me in check."

"Damn right I do," I say, putting the flour down. "No heavy lifting, got it? I don't care if you feel like Wonder Woman."

We head to the front, and Claire takes a moment to admire the pastry displays. "These look so good, Amelia. People are gonna lose their minds."

I can't help but grin. "Right? I mean, if they don't, they've got no taste."

We both laugh at the pun.

"So, who was here earlier?" she asks, raising an eyebrow.

I lean against the counter, casually dropping the bomb. "Oh, just Mrs. Anderson and Cynthia… they want us to make the wedding cake."

Claire's eyes grow wide. "Wait, the wedding cake? That's huge! A job like that could cover our expenses for a month, maybe two. You know money is no object for them."

"I know." I say, grinning. "We're talking a fancy multitier cake with all the bells and whistles. It's exciting, thinking about how much the business is really starting to take off."

Claire nods, her eyes gleaming with that ambitious fire she's always had. "Yeah, but we have to keep growing. Can't get too comfortable, you know that."

I laugh. "Don't worry, I haven't forgotten the one-year plan. We're on track."

She smirks. "Good. And don't forget there's a five-year plan, too. And a ten-year..."

I smile, remembering all the late nights we've spent talking about turning Sweet Talk into a chain of local bakeries. Big dreams, but we're getting there one step at a time. "Yeah, yeah, I'm all in for world domination."

Claire heads over to the door to flip the sign announcing we're open but stops mid-flip, her hand frozen. "What's up?" I ask, curious. She lets out a low, impressed whistle before shaking her head, a grin tugging at the corners of her mouth. "It's the neighborhood hottie."

I practically trip over myself getting to the door, and sure enough, there he is—my neighbor, looking like a freaking Greek god in motion. I say it out loud before I even realize it.

"Sexy fucking accountant."

Claire turns to me, perplexed. "What?"

Blushing, I stammer, "He's my neighbor. And that's what I call him in my head. He's got this smart, put-together style and vibe about him, especially when he wears his glasses."

Claire looks from me to him, and I can feel her assessing the situation with that knowing smirk of hers. Meanwhile, I'm watching his ass, which, in those running shorts, I can see is perfectly sculpted. I can already feel the heat rising between my legs.

Claire catches my not-so-subtle gaze and laughs. "You know, it's one thing to admire, but girl, you're straight-up eye-fucking him."

I snap out of it, my face going full-on red. "I am *not* eye-fucking him," I protest, but I can't keep a straight face.

Claire shakes her head, still laughing. "Sure, okay. You remind me of the way I used to catch myself staring at David when we first started dating. Same energy."

"Okay, fine," I admit, groaning. "Maybe I was eyeing him a little."

Claire chuckles. "Just make sure you don't drool on the pastries. That could be bad for business."

Claire smirks but then pauses, tilting her head as she gives Sexy Accountant another glance. "He's definitely a looker. He's got to be what, mid-forties? Maybe late forties?"

I nod, taking another sip of my now-cold coffee. "Yeah, I'm thinking the same. I've never been one to drool over older guys, but he's definitely an exception."

Claire places her finger on her chin in that thoughtful way she always does when something's cooking in her brain.

I raise an eyebrow at her. "Alright, spill it. What's going on in that head of yours?"

Claire quirks an eyebrow and asks, "So, you said he was your neighbor. Where does this guy live specifically?"

I shrug, trying to play it cool. "In that huge house right across the street. Why?"

Before I can even blink, Claire's grinning like a maniac and rushing over to the counter. She grabs a pastry box and starts loading it up with muffins.

"Uh, what are you doing?" I ask, suddenly feeling nervous as hell.

Claire looks up, still grinning. "If you like this guy, you can't just be drooling over him from the sidelines. Get out there and show him what's up!"

My stomach flips. "No way! There's no way I can do that," I say, feeling the panic rise as she continues filling the box.

"Why not?" Claire shoots back. "Bring him a little box of treats, and who knows? Maybe it'll get him thinking about something else he might want to snack on."

I burst out laughing. "You're awful! I can't believe you just said that."

She shrugs, totally unbothered. "Just saying, babe. Sometimes you have to be a little proactive."

She finishes packing up the muffins, seals the box, and ties it shut with a little ribbon. The whole thing looks way too cute and innocent for the dirty thoughts running through my head.

I'm still not entirely sure I want to do this, even though the idea is kind of thrilling. I glance over my shoulder and see some of our regulars heading for the front door. Claire catches the look and nudges me. "Girl, get moving! If you hurry over there now and come right back, you'll still make it in time for the morning rush."

"But what if he answers the door?" I ask, feeling the nerves bubbling up in my chest. My palms are starting to sweat at the thought of actually talking to him face to face.

Claire's grin is downright devious. "Then I'll be more than happy to cover for you if you need a little extra time." She winks, and I let out a half-nervous, half-excited squeal.

"Okay, okay, I'm going," I say, grabbing the box of muffins. My heart is already racing, and it only beats faster as I hurry out the front door, muffin box clutched to my chest like it's a damn life raft.

The cool morning air hits me as I walk down the street, but it does nothing to calm the storm of nerves and excitement swirling inside me. I seriously cannot believe I'm about to do this.

As I turn the corner onto my block, I catch sight of him just as he slips inside his house. My heart skips a beat—I was kind of hoping he wasn't home yet.

I stop a few feet away, psyching myself up for what I'm about to do. "Okay," I mutter to myself, clutching the muffin box a little tighter. "Just drop it off, say something flirty, and then run."

I stand at the front door and take a deep breath.

I ring the doorbell and wait, trying not to squeeze the box so hard that I crush the pastries inside. After what seems like a full minute, there is still no answer. Glancing around, I spot a small table for packages near the door. "Okay, just leave it and go," I tell myself. As I bend down to set the muffin box on the table, I notice a big envelope sitting there, half-hidden under some junk mail.

Not wanting to squish whatever's inside, I move the envelope carefully and place the box down before setting the envelope neatly on top without turning it over. Who his mail comes from is none of my business.

Perfect. I take a step back to admire my handiwork. Mission accomplished. Now, all I have to do is get out of here before my mind wanders back into the gutter.

I turn to leave, but something stops me. I glance back at the box. Normally, we seal our boxes with one of our cute little logo stickers, making it clear it's from Sweet Talk. But Claire, in her rush, tied it up with ribbon, forgetting the sticker, so the box is just blank. No way Sexy Accountant's going to know where these muffins are from.

Sighing, I pull out the pen from my apron and scribble a quick note on top of the box:

Hey, neighbor! Thought you might enjoy some treats from down the street. — Amelia from Sweet Talk

I head back down the steps, closing the gate behind me. With my heart still racing from this whole ridiculous muffin delivery, I make my way back to the bakery, trying to wrap my head around what just happened, wondering if I'll ever hear from Mr. Sexy Accountant.

CHAPTER 4

MELOR

The chime from the front door echoes through the house, but I'm not in the mood for company. Whoever it is can wait or, better yet, go away.

Instead, I strip off my sweat-soaked running clothes, tossing them aside as I make my way to the shower. The sleek tiles are cold under my feet, but I welcome the chill.

On my way, I catch my reflection in the mirror. Broad shoulders, lean muscle, and a body still in fighting shape. The scars tell stories I don't care to relive—one across my side from a knife fight in Moscow, another on my arm, a bullet that came a little too close. The Bratva tattoos etched into my skin are a permanent reminder of who I was, and who I still am beneath the surface.

I frown at my image. I've been working too much lately—meetings, deals, logistics—so much that I've been slacking on the gym, even though it's right in the basement. No excuses. I can't afford to slip up, not in the world I live in.

I shake my head and step into the shower. The hot water hits my skin, rinsing away the grime from the run, but not the tension that's settled in my shoulders. Steam fills the space, but my mind is elsewhere, already working through the next items on my list that I need to handle.

No distractions. Not now.

I've got a meeting with Borealis Tech—a billion-dollar corporation drowning in their own incompetence. They've been hacked three times in the past six months, and now they're desperate enough to finally come to me. No doubt they cut corners and went with some low-rent cybersecurity firm instead of the best. And now, they're paying for it.

The deal will be mine. That's all that matters.

I finish up in the shower, steam swirling around me as I dry off. I pull on a crisp, tailored off-white shirt, open at the collar, and pair it with dark grey slacks. Sharp, business-casual, but with enough edge to remind them who they're dealing with.

I head down the stairs to the first floor, the sound of my footsteps echoing in the quiet expanse of the house. My thoughts drift back to the doorbell earlier. Whoever it was, they're probably long gone by now. I can always check the camera footage later if necessary. But as I open the front door, something unexpected catches my eye.

A box.

Strange.

On top of it sits an envelope, but my attention turns to a little note scribbled across the top of the box. I read it, the corner of my mouth twitching in mild amusement, though I remain cautious. It's from one of the girls at Sweet Talk, the bakery I jog past now and then. I don't frequent places like that, but I've noticed them working inside. And I know right away which girl this is from.

There are only two women who run the place. One of them is heavily pregnant, which leaves the other—the one I've caught sneaking glances at me more than once from across the street.

She's hard to miss. Shoulder-length blonde hair that falls in loose waves, striking green eyes that always seem to linger a second too long, and pale skin that practically glows under the sunlight. Short, curvy in all the right ways. Sexy enough that I've got a clear image of her in my mind, and just thinking about her now makes my cock twitch.

Still, this is unexpected, and I don't trust it.

I don't open the box. Instead, I set it and the envelope inside the house and prepare to head out. I'll deal with it later. Right now, I have more important things to handle.

I'm halfway out the door when curiosity gets the best of me. I pause, then head back inside, eyes on the box. With a slow tug, I untie the ribbon and lift the lid.

Sure enough, inside are artfully arranged muffins, still warm. The smell of fresh-baked goods hits me hard—sugar, cinnamon, a hint of something fruity. My stomach grumbles in response, but I know better than to devour one before a meeting. I don't need a sugar rush when I'm closing a major deal.

I grab my keys and head out, locking the door behind me. As I descend the steps, my eyes flick across the street to the neighbor's house, her house. I've seen her more than a few times, often lingering near the window or porch when I jog by, always watching. The idea of her being interested in me amuses me more than it should.

I smirk to myself, sliding into the driver's seat of my car. I'll deal with her—and the box—later. Right now, there's business to take care of. And I never mix pleasure with business.

Not yet anyway.

The drive home is uneventful. I have the top down on my car, the cool San Francisco breeze igniting my senses. I cruise through the Financial District, skyscrapers looming above, reflecting the late afternoon sun. The streets are buzzing with suits and tourists, but I keep my eyes forward, one hand on the wheel, feeling the wind ripple through my shirt.

The meeting went exactly as expected. Borealis Tech practically begged for my services; desperation written all over their faces. All I have to do is build them an impenetrable security system. Easy enough. Every firewall I create is bulletproof, not just because I'm good at what I do but because failure isn't an option. Not for me.

As I weave through traffic, I reflect on how far I've come. A career in cybersecurity was never part of the plan, but after everything that happened with the Bratva, I needed a change. Something cleaner, smarter. And so far, it's been satisfying. There's a thrill in creating something unbreakable. Something only *I* control.

As soon as I pull in the driveway, my eyes absently flick over to the house across the street. For some reason, I catch myself hoping she's there, standing at her window or outside on the porch, just so I could catch another glimpse of her. I stop myself, shaking my head.

Don't be ridiculous. She's just a girl. A curious, sweet little distraction.

I remind myself that distractions lead to mistakes. And mistakes are something I don't make.

I park in the secure garage below my house, the heavy metal door sliding shut behind me. Every inch of my house is secured—cameras, reinforced doors, alarms. A fortress, just like I need it to be. I step out of the car, my footsteps echoing in the expanse of the garage, and make my way inside.

Climbing the stairs to my office, I glance around my place—simple, clean, and above all, private. When I reach the office, I take a moment to admire the view from my desk. The Mission District, with its mix of old Victorian houses and modern condos, stretches out in front of me. The sun's starting to dip lower, casting a golden glow over the city.

I pour myself a small glass of whiskey, savoring the burn as I sit down behind my computer. The first thing I do is check my account. Sure enough, there's a deposit from Borealis Tech—$1.2 million for a month's work. Half of it paid now, the balance when the firewall is complete.

I lean back, sipping my whiskey, feeling that satisfying burn settle in. This is what I live for—control, power, success.

Glass in hand, I head downstairs. As I pass the kitchen, my eyes fall on the box of muffins. My stomach grumbles, and I realize I haven't eaten since this morning. Maybe it's time to see what my neighbor left for me.

The muffins are impressive, decorated with care. My eyes land on one that looks like it's bursting with blueberries, the sugar crystal glaze catching the light. I take a bite, and *holy shit*. The taste hits me so hard I nearly moan. Soft, sweet, with just the right balance of tartness from the blueberries and the buttery crumble on top. I take another bite, then another, losing control in a way I rarely do. The muffin isn't just good, it's incredible. I can only imagine how perfect it must've been fresh out of the oven this morning. I cheated myself by waiting this long.

I savor one more bite, my appetite barely restrained, when the envelope that was on top of the box catches my eye. I set the half-eaten muffin down, curiosity piquing as I tear open the envelope. Pictures. I flip through the first few and my breath hitches.

The pictures are of my neighbor. Professionally done shots of her in a holiday-themed outfit. In the first, she's standing with her hands on her hips, a sultry smile on her face, wearing a tight green velvet costume that hugs her curves in all the right ways. The hem is so short it barely covers her thighs. As I flip through, the poses become more provocative —legs crossed, back arched, each photo revealing a little more skin.

One shows her sitting, legs spread just enough to tease, her chest pushed forward, the neckline plunging dangerously low. In another, she's tugging at her top, slipping it off one shoulder, exposing creamy skin but never quite giving it all away. The photos are in the order of a slow striptease, removing just enough clothing to drive any man insane, but always stopping short of fully revealing her body.

She's fucking sexy. Sexy enough that my cock is getting hard just looking at her.

Using all the restraint I can muster, I set the photos down, pulse racing. I flip over the envelope, searching for a clue as to why she would have sent these when she's never so much as spoken a word to me. Muffins are one thing; racy pictures are quite another.

On the front side of the envelope it's addressed to an Amelia Jameson.

I realize immediately that I've seen something I wasn't supposed to. Those photos weren't meant for me—they were delivered to my address by mistake. But one thing's clear—I'm horny as fuck. My cock is rock-hard, stiff as a spear, the images of her now burned into my brain.

I tuck the photos away, trying to get a grip on myself, but it's too late. I'm already imagining her in that tight elf outfit, and every muscle in my body is begging for release. I hurry upstairs and step into my bedroom, closing the door behind me.

Once there, I pull out my cock, already swollen and throbbing. I wrap my hand around it, stroking slowly at first. I close my eyes, letting the fantasy take over. I picture her on her knees, looking up at me with those bright green eyes, that sly, teasing smile on her lips. She's still wearing that ridiculous elf costume, her breasts barely contained in the fabric, the hem of her skirt just brushing the tops of her thighs.

She parts her lips, taking me into her mouth, slowly at first, teasing the head of my cock with her tongue, then sucking me deeper, her hands sliding up my thighs. I imagine the heat of her mouth, the way she'd relax her throat, her eyes watering as she swallows all of me.

Fuck, I can barely hold back.

I imagine the sounds of her mouth working on me—the wet, eager sucking as her lips glide up and down my shaft, her tongue swirling around the tip, then traveling down to my balls, taking one gently into her mouth, teasing me with slow licks. The thought alone nearly drives me over the edge.

In my mind, I reach down into her top, slipping my hand beneath the fabric and taking hold of one of her full tits. Her nipple is already hard against my palm, and I squeeze, feeling her moan around my cock. I pull her to her feet, turning her around and bending her over in front of me.

"You want this, don't you?" My voice is low and commanding. She nods, biting her lip, her breath coming out in shaky gasps.

She's not wearing any panties. Her pussy is pink and glistening, already wet and ready for me. I grab her hips and mount her, sliding inside her in one swift motion. She cries out, her back arching as I take her from behind. Her ass bounces against my hips, and I can feel her body trembling with every thrust.

She's moaning my name, her voice breathy, desperate. Her pussy clenches around me, so tight it feels like she's pulling me deeper with every stroke. I grip her hips harder and pound into her, the sounds of our bodies slapping together filling the room. She's close and so am I, her cries growing louder, needier.

I can feel her about to break, and I'm right there with her, holding back for only a moment longer.

"Come for me," I growl, gripping her hips even tighter, my voice commanding and low.

"Yes," she gasps, her voice shaky, desperate. "Yes, I'm so close, please..."

"Say it," I demand, thrusting deeper. "Tell me you're mine."

"I'm yours," she moans, her body trembling. "I'm yours, I'm —oh God, I'm coming!"

She breaks, her body tightening around me, gripping my cock like a vice as she shudders, coming hard. The feeling of her pulsing, squeezing me, pulls me over the edge, and I lose control. My orgasm hits like a hammer, and I erupt inside her in my mind, imagining the heat of my release filling her up, draining into her until it overflows down her thighs.

I keep thrusting until every last drop is gone, her body still quivering beneath me. The pleasure is blinding, overwhelming. I can barely hold myself together as I ride it out, feeling every inch of her as she trembles in my grip...

Just then, I snap back into reality. I'm in my bedroom, my hand still wrapped around my cock, slick with my own cum.

Fuck. I can't believe I got so carried away.

I quickly clean myself up, wiping away the mess and shaking off the fantasy. But the images from those pictures—her curves, the teasing smiles—won't leave my mind.

I know better than to let sex distract me, but right now, it's all I can think about. All I want is to see her again, to make that fantasy a reality.

I grin to myself. I'm a man who always gets what he wants.

And right now, I want her.

CHAPTER 5

AMELIA

"Done!"

The day is finally winding down.

It's 3:30, and the last of the afternoon customers have trickled out, leaving the bakery quiet except for the hum of the ovens. I'm beat, but it's the best kind of tired. The kind where you know you've killed it.

Now comes one of my favorite parts of the day: gathering up what's left for Saint Martha's, the women's shelter a couple of blocks down. It's kind of become my thing, donating whatever we don't sell. The only problem today is that we've sold so much there's barely anything left. A good problem to have, I guess, but I hate the thought of showing up nearly empty-handed.

I scan the shelves, hoping there's at least something worth taking. The display case is looking a little bare. There are a couple of blueberry scones, one pumpkin muffin, and a few cranberry-orange cookies that I'm honestly surprised didn't get snatched up.

I lean against the counter, tapping my fingers and thinking. It's not much, but I'm not about to skip the shelter run just because we had a killer day. Maybe I can whip something up really quick—anything to bulk up the offering. Those women deserve it.

I grab a box and start packing what's left, my mind already spinning with ideas of what to make.

I glance around the back, my eyes landing on a tub of cookie dough we prepped earlier. Perfect. A quick tray of chocolate chip cookies should do the trick. I grab the dough, preheat the oven, and start scooping, keeping one eye on the front door through the kitchen window.

Just as I pop the cookies in the oven, Claire walks in, rubbing her growing baby bump. "What are you up to now?"

"Whipping up some chocolate chip cookies for the women's shelter," I explain, wiping my hands on my apron. "We sold so much today, there's barely anything left. Gotta make it worth the trip."

Claire smiles, leaning against the counter. "That's sweet of you. But you know we can't always be giving away extra stock."

I pause, looking over at her. "I know, but maybe we could plan ahead and make a little extra of everything. That way, we've got plenty to donate without cutting into what we sell."

She chuckles, shaking her head. "We don't have enough overhead right now to be whipping up extra trays of pastries just to give away. It's a nice tax write-off, sure, but we're still a business."

I sigh, knowing she's right. "Yeah, I know. Just sucks we can't do more."

Claire pats my shoulder. "We'll be able to do a lot more when we grow. We just need to stick to the plan."

"I agree. But I still like doing whatever we can now. Hey," I add as an idea pops into my head. "It's getting close to Christmas. We should plan something extra nice for the shelter. You know, really make it special."

Claire's eyes light up. "I'm down for that! What are you thinking?"

We chat it out, and after some back-and-forth, we strike a deal: Come Christmas, we'll bake enough muffins for everyone at the shelter, plus cupcakes for the kids. It's a small way to spread some holiday cheer without breaking the bank.

"But," Claire adds with her signature I'm-the-boss grin, "starting next year, we might have to scale back on the daily drop-offs. Maybe switch to a few times a week instead of every day. Just for a while."

I sigh but I know she's right. "Yeah, okay. I get it. Gotta be realistic."

She pats her bump with a satisfied smile. "Exactly. But Christmas? We're going all out."

Then her grin turns a little too mischievous for my liking. "Speaking of Christmas, did you get the boudoir photos?"

My cheeks heat up even though I'm trying to play it cool. "Don't remind me. I still can't believe I let you talk me into something so outrageous."

Claire laughs. "You needed a little spice in your life!"

The boudoir shoot had been her brilliant idea—a birthday gift she insisted I couldn't refuse.

Claire smirks. "Look, I love that you're so committed to the bakery, but babe, you've let your love life fall off the face of the earth. Those photos were to, you know, reinvigorate things. Remind you that you're a beautiful, sexy woman who deserves to feel like one."

I roll my eyes, but I can't help smiling. "Yeah, I know."

"And it worked, right? Didn't you feel sexy?"

I shrug, feeling my face warm up a little. "I guess. The photographer knew what she was doing. She managed to make me feel pretty damn good, honestly."

Claire's eyes sparkle. "Told ya!"

I suddenly remember it's been a few weeks since the shoot. "Actually, the photos should be here by now. I should've gotten them already."

Frowning, I pull out my phone, checking my email and tracking the package. My stomach twists as I see the status.

"Delivered," I mutter. "Weird, I haven't gotten them yet."

A ding snaps me out of my thoughts, and I rush over to the oven. The cookies look amazing—golden brown with gooey chocolate chips.

"Perfect," I say, "but they'll need to cool a bit before I can take them over to the shelter."

Claire peeks over my shoulder. "Why don't you throw them on a paper plate? They'll cool off on the walk over."

"Genius. Why didn't I think of that?"

She hands me the box with the rest of the leftovers already packed up. "Here. Tell the staff I said hi, okay?"

"Will do!" I grab the plate of cookies and the boxed-up treats, balancing them as I head for the door.

The walk to the shelter is quick, and when I arrive, I make sure to tell the staff to grab a cookie before they're all gone.

"I made plenty, so don't be shy," I say with a wink. They thank me and after some quick goodbyes, I'm on my way back, my mind still on those damn photos.

Upon arriving home, I unlock the door to my small but cozy place, and step inside. It's nothing fancy but I love it—soft pastel walls, a small sectional couch, and a killer view of the city— the perfect space for me to unwind after a long day at the bakery.

I toss my bag aside, grab my laptop, and settle onto the couch. Time to figure out what the hell happened to those photos.

I open my laptop and check the email. Sure enough, it says the photos were delivered yesterday. But I check my mail every day, and there's been nothing. My eyes scan the email again, and that's when I spot it.

No. No, no, no.

I live at 719. The photos were delivered to 718.

My stomach drops. I grab my phone and call Claire, pacing around the living room while I wait for her to pick up. On the second ring, she does. "What's up?"

"Claire!" I practically shout. "Those boudoir photos? They were sent to the wrong address!"

"Okay?" she says, sounding like she doesn't see the problem. "Calm down, it's not the end of the world."

"Not the end of the world? Claire, someone out there has a packet of racy photos of me in a sexy elf costume! What if they end up in the wrong hands and get plastered all over the internet? They could go viral!"

She laughs, completely unfazed. "Relax, Am. Look up the address and see where it is."

I go cold as I realize who it is. "I don't need to look it up." I swallow hard. "718 is right across the street. Mr. Sexy Accountant himself."

There's a beat of silence before Claire bursts out laughing. "Oh, shit. That's one way to make an impression!"

"It's not funny, Claire," I grumble.

Claire's laughter turns into a chuckle. "Okay, okay, I'll go easy on you. But come on, you gotta admit it's a *little* funny."

I throw myself onto the couch, burying my face in a pillow. "I have to figure out what to do."

Then it hits me hard, like ice water running down my spine. "What if he opened it and looked at the pictures?" My voice is barely above a whisper but the panic in it is screaming.

Claire doesn't miss a beat. "If he did, he probably has a huge boner."

I roll onto my back, staring at the ceiling, feeling the weight of the world on my chest. "I can't deal with this right now."

Claire's voice softens. "Look, he probably didn't open it. It was addressed to you, right? Maybe he just set them aside, figuring it was a mistake and plans to bring them over to you later."

"Yeah, maybe."

"Before you start imagining your sexy elf pics going viral, though, just go over and talk to him. Explain the mix-up. It's a little embarrassing, but that's life."

I sigh, knowing she's right. "I guess so. I mean, it could be worse, right?"

"Exactly. It's not like you're the first person to have a package sent to the wrong address."

"Yeah, but how many have accidentally sent provocative photos to their hot neighbor?"

"Hey, you might get lucky out of the deal."

"Shut your trap," I snap, though I can't help but laugh a little through the panic.

"Girl, you definitely need to get laid," she teases, and I can practically hear her smirking.

I sigh dramatically. "Okay, I'm going over there. I'll just face the music, I guess."

We hang up after she makes me promise to call her back afterward and tell her how it goes. I toss my phone on the couch, nerves frayed. But then, as I stand up, a horrifying realization hits me like a ton of bricks.

The envelope I saw at my neighbor's this morning most likely had my photos in it. And I had literally placed it on top of the muffin box, like it was part of the gift.

My heart skips a beat, and I freeze, staring out the window at his house. Did I unknowingly giftwrap my sexy elf photos and hand-deliver them like some kind of perverted Secret Santa?

I swallow hard, my heart racing. No backing out now. I have to fix this.

Taking a deep breath, I stare across the street, trying to psych myself up. Then, before I can change my mind, I grab my coat, throw it on, and head over.

CHAPTER 6

MELOR

God, she's fucking sexy.

I can't stop looking at the pictures.

Each one is a perfect tease, a slow unraveling of her body, the kind of images that stick with you. I almost want to burn them into my memory—every curve, every sly smile, every inch of pale skin. My cock stirs again as I sip my whiskey.

Just as I'm about to start from the beginning again, my phone buzzes with a notification from my Ring cam, followed by a soft chime at the front door. I pick up the phone and swipe to the camera feed, grinning as her image pops up on the screen.

Perfect.

I toss the photos back into the envelope, attempting to seal it, but the glue's dried up, leaving it half-open. Nothing I can do about that now. I leave the envelope on my desk and set down my glass, descending the stairs and striding to the front door with purpose.

When I reach the door and pull it open, her scent hits me instantly— sugar and cinnamon—a sweetness that mixes perfectly with the sight of her. Her face is even more angelic in person, and for a moment, I'm nearly speechless.

The pictures were incredible, but nothing compares to the real woman.

I catch her eyes as they scan down my body, taking in my frame. She clears her throat, trying to compose herself, but I know I've had an effect on her, just as she's had on me.

Good.

"Hi," she starts, her voice a little shaky. "I'm Amelia. I'm, um, your neighbor." She tilts her head backward, toward the small house across the street.

"Melor," I respond, my voice calm and deep as I extend my hand. Hers is soft and small as she slips it into mine for a brief shake, but the electricity between us is immediate.

"How can I help you?" I ask, playing dumb even though I know exactly why she's here.

She takes a deep breath, clearly summoning up her courage. "An envelope addressed to me was delivered here by mistake. Did you happen to get it yet?"

I lean against the doorframe, tilting my head slightly, amusement tugging at the corners of my mouth. "An envelope?"

She has no idea just how much I already know.

Her voice is like music—smooth, harmonious, and laced with a softness that makes me wonder how she'd sound if I were to seduce her, make her mine.

She's dressed simply in a band t-shirt, a worn jean jacket, and tight black jeans that hug her curves. Nothing extravagant, but enough to make my cock stir to life again.

"I did receive a large envelope," I admit, my eyes holding hers, "and I opened it by mistake."

Her face flushes immediately, the color moving from her cheeks to her neck in a wave of embarrassment. She looks down for a second, as if debating whether to run or face this head-on.

"Did you... did you look at the contents?"

"I did, as a matter of fact. Not intentionally, of course."

I nod slowly, watching as her blush deepens, spreading across her face like wildfire. I don't think I've ever seen anything so sexy. There's something about her vulnerability in this moment that has my blood pumping faster, my body reacting instinctively.

"Not intentionally?"

"It was on the box you left earlier. Naturally, I thought it was part of the gift."

"Naturally," she echoes.

"The envelope is in my office," I say, my voice calm though there's a darker edge to it now. I'm tempted to see just how far this little game will go. She has no idea what kind of effect she's having on me, or maybe she does. Either way, one thing's for sure—I'm not letting her leave without getting a little closer.

"Come on in," I say, stepping aside as I gesture for her to come through the door. She hesitates for a second, but then nods and steps past me, her scent—sweet and warm—wrapping around me like a drug. It's impossible not to notice the way her hips sway with every step, how round and curvy her ass is, just like the rest of her.

One glance is all it takes. The image of her bent over, completely nude, her skin flushed as I prepare to take her from behind flashes through my mind. It's the same fantasy that had me hard just hours ago. And I'm right there again, trying to hold back the primal urge she's stirring in me.

She moves into the house, glancing back briefly. "Just so you know, my best friend knows where I am."

Her voice is steady but there's a layer of nervousness in her tone. She's smart. She's not just walking into a stranger's home without covering her bases. I like that. She's careful, cautious.

"Noted," I respond, my voice low, watching her as she looks around. She takes in the minimalist style of the place—clean lines, dark furniture, everything intentionally placed.

"Nice place," she says.

"Thanks."

I lead her up the stairs, her soft footsteps following behind me. The tension between us seems to get heavier with each step. I stop outside the door to my office and gesture toward the desk.

"Like I said, they were sitting right on top of the box of muffins, so I assumed they were part of the gift."

I notice her shoulders tense up as she shifts her stance, but she forces a small smile.

"It's fine, really. I can see how you'd be confused. It was my fault anyway—I must've put the wrong house number on the order form."

She steps into the office, her eyes widening slightly as she takes in the room. Dark wood, high-tech monitors, and a wall of glass that overlooks the city. I can see the impression it's making on her, the awe she's trying to hide.

"Nice setup," she says, clearly impressed. "What do you do?"

"Cybersecurity," I reply, keeping my tone casual. I don't give any more away than I need to.

I guide her to the desk, where the envelope sits neatly. "Here," I say, gesturing to it. "Your photos."

She looks down at the envelope, her fingers brushing over it for a moment before she picks it up, visibly relieved. I can sense her nerves, but there's curiosity there, too.

"God, I had these horrible thoughts running through my head. Like some perv finding them and putting them all over the internet or something."

I chuckle, leaning casually against the desk. "You've got nothing to worry about with me. But you're right, there are plenty of sickos out there. Wouldn't blame you for thinking the worst."

She holds the envelope tight to her chest, pressing it against her breasts in a way that naturally draws my attention.

"Look," I say, stepping back a little, "no need to rush. We may not have been able to choose the circumstances of our first meeting, but now that you're here, how about a drink? We can at least be friendly neighbors."

She hesitates for a moment but then nods. "Sure, why not."

I pour her a glass of whiskey, watching as she takes it with a polite smile, barely sipping it once it's in her hands.

I study her, taking in the way she moves, how she carries herself, especially in an uncomfortable situation like this. She's fascinating. She's different from most people I meet in a way that she has no idea.

And I want to see more.

CHAPTER 7

AMELIA

"So... did you look at, um, *all* of the pictures?"

I'm trying to sound casual, feeling anything but.

Melor seems amused, his lips curving into that little half-smirk that's starting to drive me wild. He leans back slightly, all relaxed and in control.

"Yes," he says, his voice smooth, leaving it at that. No further elaboration. Not even a hint of what he thought about them.

I slowly sip my whiskey, trying to play it cool. I got what I came for so there's really no reason for me to sit here awkwardly with a man who melts my panties with a single look.

Right?

Just as I'm about to make up an excuse to go, Melor speaks. "Can I ask you something?"

"Sure," I reply, swallowing hard.

He tilts his head, studying me with those intense, dark eyes. "Why did you pose for the pictures? Were they for a boyfriend or perhaps husband?"

His button-down shirt is undone just enough to show off a glimpse of his pecs, and it's taking everything in me not to stare. My heart races as I try to keep it together.

"No. No boyfriend or husband. They were kind of a gift to myself," I say, blushing. Why does answering him feel like I'm admitting something way more personal than it is?

"They were a gift from my best friend," I continue, rambling like I always do when I'm nervous. "You know, just for fun. To remind me that I'm a woman with needs."

As the words leave my mouth, I freeze, realizing I'm oversharing. Like, *majorly* oversharing.

Melor chuckles, clearly enjoying this way too much. His amusement only makes me squirm more, and I'm hoping that my face isn't completely red from embarrassment at this point.

"Did it work?"

I blink. "Did what work?"

"Did they make you feel sexy?"

His words send my pulse racing, and I can feel my pussy clench involuntarily. The way he says it, so casually yet so full of innuendo, makes my whole body heat up.

"Well, kind of," I manage, my voice barely above a whisper.

He leans in just slightly, those dark eyes watching me. "Did you have fun?"

The question is loaded with meaning, and I know exactly what he's getting at. I clear my throat, trying to stay composed. "Not the kind of fun I wanted to have," I admit, surprising myself with how easily I'm playing along.

This man has me tangled in his words, and it's both terrifying and thrilling.

I can't believe I'm flirting with him like this. I don't even know him, and yet here I am, having a conversation with him knowing full well he's seen me in vulnerable poses nearly naked. There's no denying it—he brings something out in me I didn't even realize was there.

I clear my throat, desperate for a change in topic. "So, um… did you like the muffins?"

He chuckles again. "Yes, they were amazing."

I raise an eyebrow, glancing over him. "You don't look like the kind of guy who lets carbs come anywhere near him."

His lips curl into an amused smirk. "I like to indulge every now and then. Life wouldn't be nearly as fun without the occasional indulgence."

His eyes roam over me as he says it, making his meaning very clear. My breath catches, and my heart feels like it's going to explode right out of my chest. The room suddenly feels ten degrees warmer, and I'm fighting the urge to squirm under his gaze.

"Well," I manage, trying to keep my cool, "glad I could satisfy some indulgence for you."

He watches me like a predator sizing up its prey, and I'm not sure whether I want to run or let him catch me.

"I have to admit something," he says, his voice low and husky. "Those pictures? They were the sexiest damn things I've ever seen."

My heart skips a beat, and I can feel the heat rising in my cheeks again. "Well," I stammer, searching for something to say, "I never would've guessed you had a thing for elves."

He chuckles, that deep, rumbling sound that makes my skin tingle. "I didn't. Until I saw you dressed up as one."

I blush harder, biting my lip as I mumble, "Thanks," unsure what else to say. I can feel the weight of his gaze, as if he's undressing me with his eyes, and while there's a part of me that enjoys it way more than I should, another part of me is panicking. I'm not sure I'm ready for where this conversation's heading.

So, I move, shifting slightly as if to make my exit. "Well, I should probably—"

"Stay for dinner," he interrupts, stopping me mid-sentence. His words hang in the air, and I can't tell if he's being polite or if there's something more behind the offer.

"Just dinner. I'd like to get to know you."

I take another sip of my drink, trying to sort through the mess in my head. The tension, the flirting, the way my body responds to him.

Should I stay?

"Sure. Dinner sounds nice."

"Wonderful," he says with a smooth smile, then gestures for me to follow. He heads out of the office, and I follow, empty glass in hand.

As I walk through his house, I take in the space around me. It's all clean lines and minimalist decor, but there are little flourishes here and there—classic art pieces on the walls, a few sculptures that look way too expensive to be just for show.

There's a sense of control, of purpose, in every part of his home. There's no sign of anyone else living here.

We enter the kitchen, and I'm once again struck by how spotless and spacious it is. White countertops, stainless steel appliances—everything looks like it's barely been used. He motions for me to sit at the island while he gets started on dinner.

"Won't take long," he assures me. "It's a classic beef stroganoff, my personal favorite."

I watch as he moves around the kitchen with precision, grabbing ingredients from the fridge and setting them on the counter. His movements are confident and practiced.

"So," I ask, curiosity finally getting the best of me, "where are you from?"

"Russia," he says, and I catch the faintest trace of an accent in his words. Just a hint, like a whisper from the past.

I watch as he starts prepping the ingredients, chopping onions, and tossing butter into the pan with a casual ease. "What're you doing there?" I ask, more curious than I'd like to admit. He doesn't mind the question, though. In fact, he seems to enjoy it.

"Making the sauce," he says, glancing at me with a half-smile. "Onions, garlic, some sour cream to bring it together. Nothing too complicated."

I tilt my head. "I'm a baker. I like to watch how other culinary aficionados work."

He chuckles, flipping the onions in the pan like it's second nature. "You'll have to grade my technique, then. But don't expect too much—I wouldn't call myself a chef. Barely an amateur, really."

I watch him for a second, his movements far too smooth, too effortless, for someone who claims to be an amateur. He's not even glancing at a recipe—just working from memory, like someone who's done this a hundred times. He grabs a knife, spinning it in his hand with a quick, precise flourish before chopping the mushrooms.

The control he has over that blade is almost *too* skilled.

I raise an eyebrow. "Muscle memory?"

He meets my gaze, holding it for a moment longer than necessary, his lips twitching into a knowing smirk. "Exactly. Comes in handy."

Maybe I'm being crazy, but there's something about the way he handles that knife that tells me he knows how to use it for more than just cooking.

The kitchen is starting to smell incredible, the rich aroma of butter, garlic, and onions filling the air. My eyes drift to Melor's huge, powerful hands, the way they move so confidently as he works. I start imagining what those hands would feel like on my body, sliding between my legs.

Before I get too carried away, he glances over his shoulder at me. "Would you grab a bottle of wine from the pantry?" he asks, gesturing toward a door on the far side of the kitchen.

I nod, sliding off the stool. "Sure, but full disclosure—I know nothing about wine."

He chuckles, wiping his hands before following me into the oversized pantry. The space is almost as big as my entire kitchen, several shelves lined with expensive bottles. I glance around, trying not to look completely lost.

"What do you prefer?" he asks, scanning the labels.

"Uh... box wine?" I joke, then immediately feel my face heat up.

Oh my God, why did I say that?

He doesn't miss a beat, laughing softly. "Does your box come in red or white?"

I feel the heat spread from my cheeks down my neck.

"Red."

CHAPTER 8

MELOR

I'm completely charmed by her.

She's the opposite of pretentious, and after the women I've dated in the past, it's refreshing. There's something genuine about her, a little bit shy but not in a way that feels forced—like she's still figuring me out as well as herself.

I find myself glancing up from the stove, watching her as she watches me. The way she nervously fidgets with the hem of her shirt, or how she bites her lip when she thinks I'm not looking—it's adorable.

"So," I say, breaking the comfortable silence, "what do you like best about baking?"

She blinks as if caught off guard, but then her eyes light up. "I don't know, there's something magical about it. You take a bunch of simple ingredients—flour, sugar, butter—and with the right care, you turn them into something that makes people happy. I love how it's both science and art. You have to be precise, but there's room to be creative, too."

Her passion spills out in her words, and I can't help but be drawn to it. So many people lack passion, drifting through life without truly caring about what they do. She's different. It's rare.

Once dinner's ready, I plate up the beef stroganoff and place the dishes on the counter.

"Could you grab the wine and two glasses from the cupboard?" I ask, nodding toward the kitchen cabinet. "We'll take everything to the dining room."

She smiles, grabbing the bottle and glasses, and I watch her, as if under a spell.

We walk into the dining room, plates in hand, and I grab a loaf of bread from the kitchen counter on the way. The room is as pristine as ever, and I find myself admitting something I rarely do.

"I've never actually used this room for anything except business meetings."

She laughs, the sound light and airy. "That's a shame. It's beautiful in here."

She's right, of course. The dining room is big and spacious, with high ceilings and tall windows that overlook the back garden. The sweeping view of the meticulously kept greenery outside adds a touch of serenity to the room. A long, dark wood table stretches out before us, perfectly polished, surrounded by plush chairs that have barely been sat in.

We sit down and get settled in and I pour the wine. I hold my glass up, meeting her eyes.

"To unexpected company," I say. It feels appropriate. This night wasn't planned but I'm already enjoying it more than I anticipated.

"To unexpected company," she repeats with a smile, clinking her glass against mine.

We each take a sip, then she digs into the beef stroganoff. After her first bite her eyes widen, and she makes a soft, satisfied sound.

"Oh my God, this is amazing! I'm definitely going to need the recipe."

I smile, watching her enjoy the meal. "I'm glad you like it."

She takes a few more bites, savoring each one before she washes it down with a sip of wine. Then, she looks at me, curiosity in her eyes.

"So, you're in cybersecurity?"

I pause, realizing I'm not used to people asking me about my work. When they do, it's never for personal interest. Still, there's no harm in answering.

"I am. And I secured a solid client today," I respond.

She smiles, genuine and warm. "Congrats. That's awesome. Do you enjoy what you do?"

I nod, keeping my response brief. "I do. It's a good feeling, knowing you're providing security for others." I take another sip of my wine, hesitating slightly before adding, "It's not too different from what I did before."

I scold myself internally the second the words leave my mouth.

Careful.

I don't talk about my past, and this isn't the moment to start. I can feel her gaze on me, and I know she's picking up on what I didn't say.

"What did you do before?" she asks, the curiosity in her voice mixed with a hint of caution.

I meet her eyes, offering a slow, deliberate smile. "I was in a more... private kind of security. More personal."

Her expression shifts to guarded intrigue. She's smart, and she knows there's more to the story. But for now, I leave it at that. Some truths aren't meant to be shared so easily.

The warm light from the sunset pours through the windows, casting a soft glow on her face. It brings out the green in her eyes, making them almost hypnotic. I find myself momentarily transfixed by her, by the way she carries herself—stunning, even in her simplicity.

"So," I ask, breaking the silence, "tell me about yourself, Amelia. Where are you from?"

She hesitates for a moment then says, "I'm from L.A. originally. Moved here after my parents passed."

"I'm sorry," I say quietly, watching her reaction closely.

She nods, offering a small, bittersweet smile. "Thanks. It was a car accident. I was away at college when it happened." She pauses, taking a sip of wine. "I guess that's part of the reason why I came to San Francisco. A fresh start, you know?"

I can relate to her. "I know what that's like. I lost my parents too. Illness took my mother, and my father followed soon after. It was like he couldn't bear to live without her."

Our eyes meet, and there's a moment of quiet understanding between us. Loss, especially at an early age, leaves scars you can't always see.

"Do you like the city?" I ask, steering the conversation toward lighter ground.

She brightens a little. "I love it here. There's something about the energy, the mix of people, the way every neighborhood feels like its own world. It's freeing."

I lean back in my chair, intrigued by how much she's opening up. "What did you do after your parents passed?"

She takes a breath. "They left me a small trust fund. Not enough to change my life, but enough to get by. I don't have any family left, so I used the money to buy my home and a space for the bakery with my best friend. We opened the bakery on the first floor, and she and her husband live upstairs." She smiles softly. "Claire's my business partner. I handle the financial and marketing side of things, and I'm also writing my first novel."

My eyebrows lift slightly at that. "A novel?"

Her face instantly flushes a deep red, and I sense I've stumbled onto something she hadn't planned to share. Her lips twitch, like she's debating how much more she wants to say.

"It's a work in progress," she admits, brushing a hand through her hair. "No details until it's ready for publishing. If it ever gets there."

I chuckle. "Fair enough. I won't press for spoilers."

She relaxes a little, but I can still see some anxiety in her eyes. She let a little secret slip, and that vulnerability only makes her more intriguing.

She grins, shifting the conversation back to me. "So, enough about me. You're from Russia? What brought you here?"

It's been so long since anyone's asked that question, I'd almost forgotten the polished lies I'd crafted over the years. "I was part of a... family business," I begin, my tone measured. "Over time, my focus shifted to cybersecurity, and I decided to go off on my own. I've always had a thing for technology."

The truth, of course, is a bit darker, but she doesn't need to know that.

I take another sip of wine, watching her reaction. She's curious, but not suspicious. "Family businesses can be stifling," I add, letting a trace of bitterness slip into my voice. "Controlling. After a while, it felt like too many strings attached."

Her eyes flicker with understanding. "So, you cashed out and moved to San Francisco to start over?"

I nod. "Exactly. A few years ago, I left it all behind. Came here for a new adventure." It's a line I've used before, but something about saying it to her feels different. I'm too close to telling her the truth.

"That's another thing we have in common," she says with a soft smile.

I meet her eyes, nodding again. "Seems so." I pause, then add, "All of my family is still back in Russia. So, for the most part, I'm alone here."

"What's your company like? Big operation?"

I shake my head. "It's just me and a few contractors. None of them live in the city, though. Mostly remote work."

"Doesn't that get lonely?"

I pause, watching her carefully. "Not at all," I reply, keeping my tone neutral.

Truth is, I don't waste time thinking about loneliness. It's a concept that doesn't fit into my world—keeping a low profile ensures survival.

She smiles. "Sounds like we're both small-business, entrepreneurial types."

A small smirk plays on my lips. "Indeed, we are."

To my surprise, I'm actually enjoying this conversation more than I thought I would. Talking with her comes easily. She's not trying to impress me or dig too deeply into things I'd rather keep hidden.

But as much as I'm intrigued by her mind, my body is demanding attention. The physical pull I feel toward her is growing stronger, nearly impossible to ignore.

A dark part of me—one I've long since learned to control—wants to take her right here, right now. I imagine her spread across the dining room table, naked and vulnerable, her legs open for me, her eyes filled with pure desire.

The thought of her writhing beneath me, giving herself over completely... is enough to make my pulse quicken.

I snap back to reality, controlling my facial expressions as I rein in the surge of lust.

Not yet, I tell myself.

She glances at me, concern in her eyes. "Are you okay?"

I blink, shaking off the dark thoughts that had taken root. I lie easily, slipping into a practiced smile. "I'm fine. Just thinking about work."

"Oh, so now I'm boring you?"

"Amelia, you could never bore me," I say with more feeling than I intended.

We finish the meal, and as she sets her fork down, she practically gushes. "Melor, seriously, that was amazing. I've never had beef stroganoff that good in my life."

"Glad you liked it."

"Liked it? I loved it. You might've missed your calling, you know. Could've been a chef."

I watch as she picks up her plate and heads to the sink, and before I know it, she's starting the dishes. I follow her, half-expecting to feel indifferent, but instead, I find myself enjoying this small, domestic moment with her.

"You don't have to help," I say, though I make no effort to stop her.

"I know," she replies, smiling over her shoulder. "But I like helping. Besides, it's the least I can do after you cooked."

We move around the kitchen easily, passing dishes, scrubbing, drying. There's an ease between us, though the tension is growing with every second. Every brush of her hand against mine, every glance, feels charged.

I hand her a dish to dry, and our fingers touch for just a moment longer than necessary. She meets my eyes, and for a brief second, neither of us moves.

"Thanks again for dinner," she says softly, breaking the silence. But her voice has a different tone now, something quieter, more vulnerable.

"Anytime," I respond.

We stand facing each other, her gaze locking onto mine, those gorgeous green eyes drawing me in like a magnet. She's so close now, and I can hear her breath catching in her throat.

I can't resist her any longer.

I step forward, my hands finding her hips, fingers digging into her soft curves as I pull her against me. She's so small in my grip, fitting perfectly against my body, and I can feel the heat radiating off her.

She doesn't say a word, doesn't try to pull away. Her lips part slightly, her breath shaky, and I close the distance, sealing her mouth with mine.

The kiss is firm and commanding, and she responds instantly, melting into me like she's been waiting for this moment just as long as I have.

CHAPTER 9

MELOR

The kiss is electric, an instant connection that sends a shiver down my spine.

I can taste the lingering notes of Pinot Noir on her lips, her tongue slipping against mine with a soft, desperate moan. My body reacts instantly and I become hard as hell, pressing my cock against her, feeling her melt into the kiss.

Suddenly, she pulls back, her chest rising and falling with quick breaths.

"I never do this," she murmurs, her voice breathless. "Never. Not even in college."

I grin, brushing a thumb across her flushed cheek.

"There's a first time for everything."

Without hesitation, we dive back in. Our lips collide, rougher this time, more urgent. Her hands slide up my chest, gripping the fabric of my shirt, pulling me closer as my tongue explores her mouth. I bite her lower lip gently, eliciting a gasp that fuels the fire burning between us.

In one smooth motion, I lift her by the waist, her legs instinctively wrapping around me as I set her on the counter. The heat between our bodies is unbearable, and I can feel her trembling as I grind against her. The friction is maddening.

I grip her thighs, pulling her closer, my need for her overtaking every thought in my head. I want her so badly it hurts.

The sound of her moans is driving me insane, making it clear that I'm giving her exactly what she wants. We kiss again, our tongues tangling, the heat building between us, until she pulls back, her breath ragged, her lips swollen.

"Something wrong?" I ask, my voice rough, my need for her nearly unbearable.

She bites her lip, glancing around the kitchen. "Are we really going to do this here? In the kitchen?"

"Fair enough," I say, sliding my hand between her thighs, rubbing her pussy through her jeans. Her breath hitches, eyes fluttering shut as she lets out a soft moan, her hips instinctively pressing forward.

I lean in, my voice low and commanding. "Let's take this upstairs."

She nods, eyes still closed, her body surrendering to the moment. I can feel her heat, her need, and as I pull her off the counter, I know this is only the beginning of what's to come.

I lift her effortlessly, her small frame fitting perfectly in my arms. There's something primal about how easily I handle her, how delicate she feels in my grasp. I throw her over my shoulder in a firefighter carry, and she lets out a soft laugh, her hands gripping my back as I ascend the stairs to my bedroom.

When we reach the bed, I toss her down, and she squeals in surprise, but the grin on her face tells me she loves every second of it. She rolls onto her back, her chest heaving, the fabric of her shirt straining against her full breasts.

We kiss again, more urgently this time, and I pull her shirt over her head, revealing her black bra, her breasts practically spilling out of it. My hands move over her skin, tracing her curves, feeling the heat radiate from her body.

"I've wanted you since the moment I opened that envelope," I murmur against her lips, my voice thick with desire.

I slide my hand into her bra, fingers wrapping around her soft breast as I tease her nipple until it hardens beneath my touch. She moans softly, her body arching into my hand, craving more. With my other hand, I reach for the button of her jeans, flicking it open and pulling the zipper down in one smooth motion. She lifts her hips, helping me out, shimmying out of her jeans with a bit of playful wriggling.

Her panties don't match the black bra, simple, light blue cotton, unexpectedly cute and sexy in their own way. I let my eyes linger, taking in every inch of her.

"You're so fucking sexy," I growl, watching her blush deepen as it spreads down her neck.

Her hand moves to my slacks, fingers grazing over the bulge. She rubs me through the fabric, making me harder with every stroke. I growl low in my throat as I press my hand against her panties, feeling the heat, the wetness already soaking through the cotton.

"Look at you," I murmur, my voice dark and commanding. "You're soaked, aren't you? So fucking wet for me."

She lets out a small whimper as I rub her clit through the fabric, her hips rolling instinctively into my hand. "Yes," she breathes, barely able to get the word out.

"You like that?" I push harder, the pressure making her gasp. "You're going to come for me, aren't you? But not yet."

Her response is a desperate moan, her body completely under my control.

I slip my fingers beneath her panties, feeling the soft heat of her skin, teasing her wet lips before sliding two fingers inside her soaked pussy. She's tight, and when I press into her, she bucks hard against my hand, her body desperate for more. I keep my thumb on her clit, rubbing slow circles, making her gasp into my mouth as we kiss, deeper and more frantic with every second.

Her moans grow louder, her breaths come quicker. She's close—I can feel it in the way her hips move, in the way her body tenses under my touch.

"You're so fucking tight," I murmur against her lips. "You love this, don't you? Being teased like this, knowing you're about to come all over my fingers."

She whimpers, nodding as her grip on my shoulders tightens. "Yes," she breathes, her voice shaky, barely able to hold back.

"Be a good girl and let go," I command, my thumb pressing harder on her clit, fingers pumping in and out of her in a slow, relentless rhythm.

"Yes... yes..." she moans, and then it happens—her body trembles, her back arches, and she comes hard around my fingers, gasping out my name. It's so fucking sexy to watch her lose control, her body shaking with pleasure as I keep my fingers deep inside her.

When she finally stills, her eyes flutter open, her chest rising and falling with ragged breaths. She smiles, her voice husky and teasing. "Now, it's your turn."

CHAPTER 10

AMELIA

I reach forward, hands still trembling, and start undoing the buttons on his shirt. As the fabric falls open, my breath hitches. Underneath, his body is insanely ripped, chiseled, and covered in tattoos.

I work on his belt, my fingers fumbling slightly in my excitement as I undo his zipper and tug down his slacks. My heart's racing as I slip my hand into his boxer briefs and pull out his enormous, thick cock—hard and already dripping just for me.

I start stroking him slowly, my eyes wide as I take in the sight of him, every inch of his giant manhood making my mouth water. I bite my lip, feeling completely out of control but loving it. I can feel his eyes on me, and then he hits me with more of that mind-blowing dirty talk.

"You like how I feel in your hand, don't you? You're going to love how I feel inside that tight, wet pussy of yours."

His words send a shiver through me, and all I can do is nod as I continue to tease him with slow, deliberate strokes. He watches me intently, dark eyes locked onto mine. After a little more teasing, he leans down and kisses me again deep and intense, the kind of kiss that sends sparks flying through my body.

Before I know it, he's positioning himself over me, his cock rubbing against my clit through my soaked panties. I gasp, my hips arching up to meet him, the sensation driving me crazy.

I'm in heaven, and I'm not sure I ever want to come back down.

He pauses, and I blink at him, panting.

"Is something wrong?"

He kisses me again, slower this time, then pulls back just enough to meet my eyes.

"We don't have to go any further than this," he says.

I smile, pulling him in for another kiss. "I want to" I whisper against his lips, no doubt in my mind that I want this.

He pulls back slightly, his gaze searching mine. "Do we need protection?"

"I'm on the pill," I tell him, breathless and aching for more. That's all he needs to hear.

With one smooth motion, he rips my panties off, positioning himself right at my entrance. I feel the head of his cock brushing against me, and I can barely breathe, every nerve ending in my body on fire.

He pushes in, slowly, stretching me as he sinks inside, and... *holy shit.*

Every inch of him feels like too much and not enough all at once.

He pushes in deeper, inch by inch, and I can feel every part of him stretching me out, filling me completely. It's like nothing I've ever felt before, his cock so thick and hard, gliding inside me with ease.

I'm on the verge of begging for more. I gasp as he bottoms out, his body pressing against mine, and I let my hands fall to his gorgeous, sculpted ass, squeezing as I pull him closer.

We kiss again, desperate, raw, and I can barely think with the way he's moving inside me. He pulls back slightly, his lips hovering near my ear as he whispers, "You feel so fucking tight around me, like you were made for me."

I moan softly, tilting my head back as he kisses my neck then moves lower, his mouth finding my breasts through my bra, sending shivers through my entire body. Every movement is slow, deliberate, like he's savoring every second.

"Faster," I manage to breathe out, my fingers digging into his back. "Deeper."

He doesn't hesitate, his hips snapping forward, pushing into me harder, faster, just like I asked. The pressure is building inside me as he picks up the pace. I can feel another orgasm already stirring, coiling tight in my stomach, just waiting to explode.

He sits up, shifting his weight and sliding a pillow under my ass, grabbing my ankles and throwing them over his shoulders. He spreads my legs wide, holding me open as he drives into me at a perfect angle. It's unreal how good it feels, every thrust hitting my G-spot.

"Come for me again," he growls, his voice low and commanding. "I want to see it. I want to *feel* it."

His words set my blood on fire, and I lose all control. My whole body tightens, and before I know it, I'm coming—hard. It's like a wave crashing over me, my back arching off the bed as I cry out, my pussy clenching around him with every pulse.

It's intense, and the way he watches me, how he knows exactly what he's doing to me, only makes it that much hotter.

After I come down from the high of my climax, he lowers himself back on top of me, kissing me slow and deep. It's like his lips are some kind of drug, and I'm already getting addicted to the way he kisses—firm, but teasing, like he knows exactly how to keep me wanting more.

He continues to thrust in and out, slow, and deep, like he wants me to feel every inch of him. And good God, do I.

Then, he takes my wrists, pinning them above my head, holding me down. I love the way he's taking control, dominating me in a way no one ever has before. It's raw and intense, but also intimate. It's like he knows what I want without me even having to say a word.

His mouth moves next to my ear, his breath hot against my skin. "Come again," he commands. "I want to feel you all over my cock."

All I can do is nod. I'm right there, teetering on the edge, ready to fall apart for him all over again. It's crazy how fast he's got me hooked but I'm too far gone to care.

His thrusts get deeper, each stroke pushing me closer to the edge. My legs wrap around him tight, and I grip his ass, pulling him in as if I can't get enough. Another orgasm slams through my body like a tidal wave. I come hard, my mind going blank with pleasure.

As I continue to tremble from my climax, I feel him coming hot and deep inside me. He groans low in my ear as he fills me, the sensations and sounds of him erupting making the moment even more intense, sexier.

I savor every second, my mouth open in a silent scream of pleasure as I give myself over to him completely. It's like nothing I've ever experienced before. I feel like I've just given a part of myself to him that I can't take back.

When it's over, he stays inside me for a minute, kissing me softly. I can feel the heat between us as he slowly slides out, and my body immediately misses him, craving that connection again.

He pulls me close, his lips finding mine, and I melt into the kiss, my hands roaming over his back. "That was..." I trail off, not even knowing how to finish the sentence.

"I know," he murmurs, his voice low and satisfied.

CHAPTER 11

AMELIA

With a sigh, I push myself up. "I should probably go. I have to be at work early tomorrow."

He smiles at me, understanding without a word, and shifts to get out of the bed, too. As much as I don't want to leave, reality's knocking, and I can't hide here forever.

Still, when he leans in and kisses me again, soft but with that lingering heat that makes my body tingle, I almost change my mind. My legs go weak thinking about how easy it'd be to stay, but with my brain screaming at me to focus, I manage to pull away.

"Thank you for tonight," I say, trying to sound casual, like what just happened wasn't completely life changing.

"Anytime."

I slip on my clothes, feeling his eyes on me the entire time. I glance over my shoulder and catch him watching me like I'm his favorite snack. His gaze makes me feel like he's memorizing every inch of me.

As I bend down to put on my shoes, a sudden crash of glass breaks the silence. My head snaps up, and we both freeze. A door creaks open loudly from downstairs, the sound unmistakable.

I look at him, eyes wide, my heart starting to race. "Are you expecting company?" I whisper, barely able to get the words out. His entire expression changes in an instant, shifting from relaxed to razor-sharp.

He puts a finger to his lips, signaling me to stay quiet. My heart's pounding so hard I'm sure whoever's downstairs can hear it. I'm frozen in place and can barely dare to breathe as he reaches into his bedside table and pulls out a gun.

He slides out of bed and pulls his clothes back on, moving with an unnerving calmness as if he's done this a million times before. I manage to find my voice, barely a whisper. "Why do you have that?"

He answers by pressing his finger to his lips again, then shoots me a look that silently tells me to stop asking questions.

"Stay here. Lock the door," he whispers. His tone is firm and authoritative, leaving no room for argument.

Without another word, he slips out of the room, moving like a shadow. I'm left standing there, my mind racing a mile a minute.

What the actual fuck is going on?

I do what he says, locking the door behind him, but my pulse is pounding, a mix of fear and confusion taking over.

As time passes, the silence becomes suffocating. My fight-or-flight instinct kicks in, and my brain is spinning out, wondering if I should call the cops, though I don't know if that would make things worse.

I press my ear against the door, straining to hear something, *anything*. But there's nothing. His house is huge, and for all I know, he could be anywhere in it. After a few agonizing seconds, I unlock the door and crack it open, sliding out into the hallway as quietly as I can.

My bare feet move silently down the hall, the tension thick enough to choke me. When I reach the landing, I finally hear voices. Melor's, and two others. The sound of their conversation makes my stomach twist into knots.

I inch closer, trying to stay hidden, but close enough to hear the exchange. One of the other men's voices breaks the stillness, sharp and accusing.

"You killed my brother."

What? My heart skips a beat. *Did he say killed?*

Melor's response is firm and composed. "I'm not a part of that life anymore."

My mind is racing, trying to make sense of it all. I press myself against the wall, realizing I've become involved in something I never expected.

Who the hell is Mellor, and what did I just get myself into?

I creep closer, staying low as the conversation becomes clearer. I can barely breathe as I listen in, trying to make sense of what's happening downstairs.

"You killed Dimitri," one of the men growls, his voice dripping with anger.

"Two years ago," a second voice adds.

There's a beat of silence before Melor speaks again, the tone of his voice sounding as if he's not fazed at all.

"I don't recall this Dimitri you speak of," he says.

"Don't recall?" the man replies incredulously. "You kill my goddamn brother, and you don't even have the fucking respect to remember him?"

"I've had a busy career," Melor says dismissively. "Faces... they have a way of blurring together after a while."

"You... you'll fucking pay for this."

I can almost *feel* Melor's apathy, the way he's so unfazed by the threat hanging in the air. Then, suddenly, I hear grunts as a scuffle breaks out, the unmistakable sound of bodies slamming into walls, fists connecting with flesh. I can hear the heavy thuds of punches and furniture scraping across the floor. It sounds like a full-on brawl is going down.

I'm frozen in place, scared out of my mind but equally terrified for Melor's safety. The sounds get louder—the grunting, the crashing—until a *clicking* noise cuts through all of it.

I'm shaking, my hands clammy as I press my body against the wall.

I can't just sit here and do nothing, I tell myself, my heart hammering in my chest.

I need to call the cops.

I pat my jean pockets and feel nothing.

Shit.

My phone's in the kitchen. Panic rises but then I remember—Melor left his phone on the table during dinner. I just need to get to it.

The sounds of the fight grow louder—more grunts, more crashing—and I'm terrified that at any second, I'm going to hear a gunshot. I force myself to move through the fear. I have to get to that phone.

I sneak down the stairs as quietly as I can, hoping to stay out of sight. My heart's racing so fast it feels like it's going to jump out of my chest. I inch closer to the bottom of the staircase, practically holding my breath.

But just as I reach the last step, a man rushes around the corner, grabbing my arm before I can react. I gasp, my heart dropping into my stomach as his grip tightens. His eyes are dark and furious, and I can feel the danger radiating off him.

Oh, fuck.

Totally by instinct, I pull back my hand and smack the guy hard across the face. The impact surprises both of us, but it's enough for him to let go of my arm. I don't think twice—I scramble back up the stairs as fast as I can, heart pounding out of control.

Behind me, I hear him swear in Russian, his voice dripping with rage.

Shit, shit, shit!

I desperately try to make it back to the bedroom, to lock the door and figure out a plan, but he's too fast. His hand clamps around my ankle, yanking me down the stairs. My body slams against each step, the pain sharp and jarring, knocks the wind out of me. I barely have time to scream before he grabs my arm again, this time so hard it feels like he's going to rip it right out of the socket.

I cry out, panic flooding my brain. I thrash and kick, trying to fight him off until cold metal presses against my throat.

"Stop," he growls, his voice rough and menacing. I feel the unmistakable shape of a gun barrel digging into my skin. I stop struggling, my body trembling, breath shallow and quick.

"Little neighbor slut," he sneers in my ear. My stomach twists in horror—he knows I'm Melor's neighbor which means he likely knows exactly where I live.

I'm frozen, completely at his mercy and terrified of what's going to happen next.

"Stop fighting or you are dead," the man hisses in my ear, his heavy Russian accent making the threat sound even more intimidating. I'm shaking, heart pounding, as I try to stay as still as possible.

Suddenly, a gunshot rings out, sharp and deafening. My blood runs cold.

The man drags me into the kitchen. My feet stumble, and I'm desperately trying to keep my balance as my body tenses with fear. When we enter the kitchen, my eyes go wide—there's a body on the floor.

But it's not Melor.

A pool of blood is slowly spreading beneath the man lying motionless on the ground, his lifeless eyes staring blankly at the ceiling. My stomach churns, and I feel like I'm going to be sick. The metallic scent of blood fills the air, and I can't tear my eyes away from the scene.

"Melor!" the man holding me shouts, his voice frantic now. "I've got your little whore. Come out now, or I'll kill her!"

His grip tightens, his panic practically vibrating off of him. I can tell he's losing control, and that terrifies me even more. He's scared and desperate, which means he might actually do something crazy. My chest tightens as I struggle to stay calm, but the fear is overwhelming.

Finally, Melor steps into the room, his presence somehow both calm and sinister. He's got his gun trained on the man holding me, blocking the only way out.

The man tightens his grip, yanking me closer and pressing the cold barrel of his gun harder into my neck. I wince, crying out as the metal digs into my skin.

"I'll shoot her," the man growls, his voice shaking a little now, his panic turning to desperation.

Melor's eyes narrow, his jaw tight, like a predator sizing up his prey. "Think carefully. You know who I am," he says. "I may be out of the life but trust me—I won't forget this."

The man behind me shifts nervously, the panic rising in his voice. "I'll kill her, and then you!"

My pulse races and I can barely breathe. Melor doesn't even flinch. His grip tightens on the gun, and I can see the tension in his muscles as he shifts his weight, like he's getting ready to move.

Is he going to shoot?

I'm about to find out.

CHAPTER 12

MELOR

"Drop the gun—now."

The man's voice is shaky but trying to sound commanding. My eyes are locked on him—and Amelia—whom he's using as a human shield. I don't know this man's name, nor the name of the one whose blood is still pooling on my kitchen floor. It doesn't matter. They made the mistake of coming into my home and threatening me—and worse, threatening *her*.

He will die tonight as well.

I can see desperation creeping into the man's eyes, the slow realization that things aren't going as planned. His original goal might have been revenge, but now he just wants to get out of here alive.

"You think I'm scared of you?" the man spits, pressing his gun into Amelia's throat, making her wince. I can see the fear in her eyes and my heart clenches. "I'll kill her right here, and I'll enjoy watching you squirm before I put a bullet between your eyes."

I feel the familiar surge of rage, a dark, deep anger that threatens to consume me. I want to take this man apart piece by piece with my bare hands, make him feel every second of his life slipping away. But I can't rush this. I have to play it smart.

One wrong move, and Amelia's dead.

I keep my gun trained on his face, my finger lightly resting on the trigger.

"Let her go," I say, my voice calm, but my eyes full of intent. "You know who I am, you know what I'm capable of. Let her go, and maybe you'll live to see another day."

The man's eyes flicker with anguish, his grip on Amelia tightening as his resolve starts to crack. He looks like he's regretting every decision that brought him to this moment.

But it's too late. He's in too deep, and I know exactly how this plays out. When people like him get scared, they panic, and panic leads to death. I've seen it too many times to count.

I keep my gun trained on his face, every fiber of my body screaming to end his life right here, right now. But I can't afford to make a mistake. The smallest misstep, and she could die. That's not an option.

The man starts inching toward the door, dragging Amelia with him. They're going to have to walk right past me to make their escape, which means he's gambling that I won't pull the trigger while he's trying to make his move.

"Do you really think I'm going to let you leave here with her?"

He flinches, his panic growing more obvious. He's making the classic mistake—believing he has control when it's actually slipping through his fingers. He's about to do something stupid, desperate, I can feel it.

"Here is what's going to happen," the man says. "You are going to leave your gun here on the counter, walk into the dining room, sit your ass down, and put your hands on the table where I can see them. Then she and I are going to leave together. Once I'm sure you're not on my ass, I will let her go."

I keep my gun steadily trained on him, my eyes never leaving his.

"That's not going to happen," I reply. "You're going to let her go, and you're going to let her go—*now*."

The man's face twists with frustration, his voice rising. "You think this is a fucking game?" He tightens his grip on Amelia and raps her on the side of the head with his gun. She lets out a sharp cry of pain, the sound piercing through me like a knife.

My rage boils over. The world narrows, and everything else fades.

I let out a slow breath, centering myself, feeling the weight of the gun in my hand. Every muscle in my body goes still. I take aim, my focus narrowing to a pinpoint.

I pull the trigger.

The man pulls Amelia down just as I fire, and the shot hits the wall, sending a puff of drywall dust into the air. I barely react, immediately taking aim for another shot. But before I can fire, he shoves Amelia toward me, using her as a shield.

She crashes into me, harder than I expected, and we both stumble into the dining room. I catch her, my arms wrapping around her instinctively, but my eyes are locked on the man bolting for the door. Over Amelia's shoulder, I see him making his escape.

I gently set Amelia down, feeling her heart pounding, but at least she's safe. That's all that matters right now. "Stay here," I murmur, and push off after him.

By the time I reach the front door, he's already outside, his feet hitting the pavement hard and fast in a desperate attempt to escape. I charge after him but he's fast—too fast. By the time I catch up, he's behind the wheel of his car, slamming the door shut with a wild look in his eyes.

I could take the shot but not here. Not in the middle of the street.

He peels out, tires screeching as his car speeds off into the night. All I can do is watch him disappear into the darkness, my jaw clenched tight.

Part of me wants to grab my motorcycle and chase him down—no doubt I'd catch up—my bike being faster and more relentless than he could ever hope to be. But I can't do that. Not with Amelia still inside, no doubt terrified after what just went down. I grit my teeth, pushing the impulse aside as I hurry back into the house.

As I pass the front door, I notice the shattered glass from the window next to it. That's how they got in. Amateurs. If they'd been professionals, they wouldn't have needed to break a window to get inside, and they certainly wouldn't have let it turn into a chaotic, botched attempt like this. The plan was sloppy— sneak in and take me out while my guard was down.

They greatly miscalculated.

But none of that matters now. Only Amelia does.

I rush into the kitchen to find her in a daze, her eyes unfocused and wide, as if she's still processing everything. Her body doesn't appear as tense and her breathing is shallow. The adrenaline is clearly wearing off.

I crouch beside her, my voice calm and quiet. "Amelia, are you okay?"

At first, she doesn't respond, but then her hands start to shake, her breath quickens, and I can tell panic is creeping in. Her breath comes in short, panicked bursts, and her eyes dart around the room, not really focusing on anything.

"Oh my God, oh my God," she mutters, her voice shaky. "He, he could've killed me. I thought I was going to die. I really thought—"

She chokes on her words, tears spilling down her cheeks as she grips the countertop like it's the only thing keeping her grounded. Her hands are trembling so badly that she starts rubbing them together as if she's trying to get rid of the fear crawling under her skin. "I can't... I can't stop shaking. I don't even know how to—" She stifles a sob, her voice breaking.

I move closer, placing my hands on her shoulders, trying to calm her down. "You're safe now," I say. "Nothing's going to happen to you. I promise."

She's struggling to pull herself together, and I can see a lump forming on her head from where the man hit her. A fresh wave of rage burns through me. That motherfucker's days are numbered. He'll regret ever laying a hand on her. But I push that anger down for now. She needs me to be focused.

"Look at me," I say firmly, and she meets my eyes. I make her follow my finger back and forth, checking for any signs of a concussion. She's shaken, but responsive. "You're okay," I tell her.

I place one hand on her back, one on her chest, guiding her through each breath. "Breathe with me. Slow and steady." She starts to match my rhythm, her breaths coming a little slower, more controlled.

Her body begins to relax but I don't let go, keeping her close.

She's slowly calming down, her breathing becoming more even as the panic fades. I'm confident she doesn't have a concussion, but I ask anyway, needing to hear it from her. "Does your head still hurt?"

She nods slightly as she wipes her eyes. "A little, but it's getting better." She looks at me with a curious expression on her face. "How do you know how to check for a concussion?"

I pause for a moment before answering. "I've had experience with them before."

Her eyes search mine before she finally blurts out, "What the hell just happened? Did you really kill someone?"

I know she has many questions, and I have to stop myself from smirking at the irony of it all. Although this night wasn't planned, once she agreed to stay for dinner, I'd hoped to keep it simple, keep things light between us. But instead, she unexpectedly got thrown into the deep end of my world without warning. She's already seen too much.

I see she's waiting for an answer, but now's not the time. Not yet. "I can explain, but for now, I think it's best if you go upstairs and sit for a moment."

She nods, and I help her to her feet, noticing that she's handling this better than most people would.

I guide her upstairs, sitting her down on the edge of my bed. Then I grab a glass from the bathroom and fill it with water, taking it to her and placing it in her hands. She drinks slowly.

Her breathing is almost back to normal though there's still tension in her eyes. I sit beside her, keeping my hand on her back, letting her know I'm here.

She's quiet for a moment as she gathers herself, then she looks up at me, her voice small but determined. "I want to go home."

I understand her need to be somewhere familiar, somewhere she deems safe. But she has no idea what she's dealing with.

"You can't," I say, my voice definitive. Her eyes widen, and I see the confusion creeping back in. "That man who got away knows where you live. He and others might come for you to get to me."

She looks away, biting her lip like she's trying to process it all, but I don't give her time to argue. "You have to stay here, Amelia. With me. I'm the only one who can keep you safe."

Her head snaps back up, eyes locking on mine, and I can see defiance in her eyes. She's not used to being told what to do, but this isn't negotiable.

I kneel in front of her and lower my voice, leaving no room for discussion. "It's the only way I can make sure nothing happens to you."

She looks like she's about to argue, but I can see the reality of the situation hitting her. She knows this isn't something she can fight alone. She's in real danger, and she knows I'm right.

"Stay with me," I repeat. "I'll keep you safe. I swear it."

CHAPTER 13

AMELIA

"No."

I'm staring into those intense, steely eyes of his, still in a total daze. There's no question he's serious—he wants to protect me, and he's definitely not used to being told no. But I'm standing firm.

He looks confused. "No?"

I cross my arms, my tone shaky but determined. "There's no way in hell I can stay with someone as dangerous as you."

His brow furrows. "Dangerous?"

"Yes, dangerous! There's a gun in your hand and a dead body in your kitchen!"

He stays calm, *too* calm for someone who just killed a man. "The body will be taken care of."

I throw my hands up. "See? This is exactly my point! You just killed someone, and you're talking about it like it's some random recycling you need to drop off. This is insane!"

The words continue to tumble out of my mouth, my voice getting louder, but I don't care.

"I just had a gun held to my head! Does that faze you at all? I've never been that close to death in my life! And now I've got trauma that I'm going to have to spend God knows how much money on therapy to unpack!"

I know I'm rambling, but I can't stop. "What the hell, Melor? I just went from a hot dinner date to witnessing a murder and being held at gunpoint! How am I supposed to process this? I'm just a baker for fuck's sake!"

He sits there calmly, saying nothing, as if he's letting me get it all off my chest first.

I'm breathing hard and my hands are shaking as I wrap up my rant. "I'm *not* staying. I'm going home, where I can pretend I didn't just live through a scene from a true crime thriller."

There's a beat of silence before he finally speaks, his voice low and unyielding.

"No."

"No?" I echo, blinking at him like he's lost his damn mind.

"No."

"You're not in charge of me."

"You can't go home," he states matter-of-factly. "You're not safe."

I scoff, crossing my arms. "I have nothing to do with any of this!"

"It doesn't matter," he counters, his eyes darkening. "They saw you with me and unfortunately that puts you in danger."

I shake my head, trying to come up with another option. "I'll stay with my best friend. Claire's—"

"That won't work," he cuts in. "It won't take much for them to figure out where you work, who your friends are. If you go to your friend's place, you're putting her and whoever else lives there in danger, too."

I open my mouth to argue, but then stop, the weight of his words hitting me like a punch to the gut. He's serious. And I know he's right.

"Whether you like it or not, Amelia, whether it's fair or not, you've been pulled into this," he says, his voice hard as stone. I can feel the anger bubbling up inside me, mixing with an awful sense of helplessness. This can't be happening. I'm trapped in a nightmare I can't wake up from.

I look up at him, narrowing my eyes. "Pulled into *what*, exactly?"

He says nothing, his jaw tight.

My frustration boils over. "No, you don't get to do that. You don't get to stay silent. I deserve to know what the hell is going on here. Who *are* you, and why do you have armed men breaking into your house, trying to kill you?"

He pauses before speaking like he's weighing how much to say. "Do you know what a Bratva is?"

I shake my head, already dreading the answer. "No."

"It's similar to what you know as the Mafia," he says, his tone flat.

"The Mafia?" I echo, the word hitting me like a slap to the face. My voice comes out shaky, my brain struggling to process what he's just said.

He nods once, his expression serious. "The Bratva. Russian organized crime. Power, control, loyalty."

I blink at him, trying to piece it together, but I can tell he's holding back. "Jesus Christ. *That's* the 'family business' you were in?" I ask.

His eyes meet mine, and I can see the weight of the answer before he even speaks.

"Yes."

I swallow hard, feeling like the floor's been ripped out from under me. "So, what, you were some kind of hitman or something?"

He doesn't answer immediately, letting the silence fill the gap between us. "There are things I can't talk about. But yes, I was part of that life. I left it years ago."

I shake my head, the pieces still not fitting. "So those guys trying to kill you? They're from this Bratva?"

He nods again, keeping his eyes on mine like he's trying to gauge how much I can handle. "They were here seeking revenge for something I did a long time ago. As I said, I've been out of that life for years, but they pulled me back in when they found me. And unfortunately, because you were here, they've pulled you into it, too."

I'm reeling, my head spinning with the revelation.

I stare at him, my heart pounding. "This is all true? No bullshit?"

"No bullshit. But listen, I need a moment," he says quietly. "I have to make a call. I promise I'll be right back."

I say nothing, still trying to wrap my head around everything that's happened as he steps away.

Melor grabs what I can only guess is a burner phone out of a dresser drawer before going out to the bedroom balcony. He shuts the sliding door behind him for some privacy. Not a chance. No way am I letting him hide more secrets from me.

As soon as his back is turned, I drain the last of my water and quietly make my way over to the door, trying to stay out of sight. I lean in, my ear close to the cool glass. His voice is low but clear enough to make out what he's saying.

"One down, one got away. I need cleanup at the house."

There's a pause, then I hear him say, "I'll find out who's behind this. No matter who they send, I'll handle it."

My blood runs cold as I listen to him speak so casually about death, violence, and revenge. It's like he's an entirely different person—someone way more dangerous than I ever could have imagined.

Suddenly, the realization of my situation sinks in. This isn't just a bad night or some weird misunderstanding. He's deep in this Bratva life, regardless of what he's told me.

And now, I'm deep in it, too.

I can't be here when they remove the body. I can't be anywhere near this.

I need to get out of here.

He's still on the phone, pacing back and forth and totally absorbed in the conversation. The eerie silver moonlight makes his silhouette look like something out of a movie, except this is real. *Too* real.

I need to go. Now.

Carefully, I slip out of the bedroom, tiptoeing my way down the stairs. My heart's pounding in my ears, and every creak of the hardwood feels like an alarm. I take a wrong turn and end up in the kitchen, staring at the dead body.

I freeze, my breath catching in my throat. I half expect the guy to move like this is some twisted nightmare where he'll stand up and come after me. But he remains still. Waxen. His body looks unreal, like a mannequin drenched in blood, the dark red pool beneath him congealed and still.

Holy shit.

I can't stop staring. I've never seen death like this—so final, so quiet. It's like the whole house is holding its breath.

Melor's voice slices through the silence. "Amelia!"

I jump, and suddenly the weight of everything comes crashing down again. I tear my eyes away from the body, the image burned into my brain, and stumble toward the front door, my mind racing.

I need to get out. I need to get out now.

But this house is huge, and I'm totally disoriented, running in the wrong direction, practically dizzy with panic.

Behind me, I hear Melor thudding down the stairs, his heavy footsteps echoing through the house. My heart's pounding as I sprint, finally finding the front door. I grab the handle, yanking on it hard, but nothing happens. The lock won't budge. It's super high-tech and complicated, and in my panic, I can't figure it out.

Shit, shit, shit!

I whip around and take off again, my feet carrying me through the maze of the first floor. I need to find a way out. My mind is a blur, and I can barely think straight. I'm running on nothing but pure adrenaline. I make it to the back door, and without stopping to think, I throw it open and rush into the garden, hoping there's a fence I can jump over or at least a place to hide.

The evening air is cool and calm, a complete contrast to the panic running through me. I run deeper into the garden, my breath ragged, when I hear his voice again, closer this time.

"Amelia!"

I turn, my stomach twisting. He's standing at the back door now, watching me. The garden suddenly feels so small. There's nowhere to go.

I stop, breathless, right in front of a massive stone fountain. It's gorgeous. Actually, the whole garden is stunning—flowers everywhere, statues tucked between trees. There's even a little stream bubbling along the path.

The beauty of it all calms me for just a second, my racing heart slowing down as I take it in. But then I hear him.

Melor appears, stepping into view, and I freeze. My emotions are a mess—I'm terrified of him, but at the same time, I feel oddly safe.

He strides toward me, those intense eyes locked on mine, and when he reaches me, his hands land firmly on my shoulders.

"You can't run. I have to protect you. You must understand that."

"I don't feel safe," I manage to whisper, though I know that's a lie. I do feel safe with him. And, incredibly, despite everything that's transpired tonight, that fact turns me on.

What the fuck is wrong with me?

His grip tightens. "I won't let anything happen to you. I promise you that."

And then, before I can say another word, his lips slam into mine.

CHAPTER 14

MELOR

I kiss her hard and she lets go.

The adrenaline is still pumping faintly through my veins from the attack, and I can feel it in her, too—whether it's from the danger or from the way we're drawn to each other, I'm not sure. Maybe it's both.

The kiss deepens, her tongue meeting mine in a wild, hungry rhythm. My hand slides down to the small of her back, pulling her tighter against me. I'm already hard as hell, my body aching for her.

"I need to be inside you," I murmur against her lips, my voice rough with need. "Right here, right now."

She moans through the kiss, her body pressing into mine, and that's all I need.

My hand slips down to her jeans, grabbing the waist and unfastening them before tugging them down. I'm beyond holding back now. The tension, the fear, the raw desire—it's all mixed into a fiery passion, and it's driving me to the edge.

She's got her hand on me, stroking me through my slacks, and damn, she knows just how to work me. The way her fingers wrap around, firm but teasing is enough to make me pause and appreciate the heat of her touch.

"You like feeling how hard I am for you, don't you?"

She bites her lip, looks up with sultry eyes, and whispers, "Maybe I just want to see how long you can last before you beg for it."

Fuck. I wasn't expecting that.

But she drops to her knees and pulls out my cock like she's been waiting for this. Her lips press against the head, soft and teasing, and electricity shoots through me. Between the danger, the exposure of being outside, and her unexpected move, I can barely contain myself.

Her tongue slowly swirls around the tip before she takes me deeper. She's not rushing it, she's savoring it. It's like her mouth was made for this, the way she sucks, just enough pressure to drive me insane, tongue flicking in all the right places.

Each time she takes me deeper, it's like the world disappears. She looks up, eyes locked on mine, and it's enough to make me forget everything but the way she's working me—relentlessly, perfectly.

Her mouth moves down my shaft, her lips soft, tongue teasing every inch. Then she's on my balls, suckling gently, kissing like she's worshiping every part of me. I feel it deep, the heat building. She's about to push me over the edge but I grab her hair, stopping her just before I lose myself.

"Up," I growl, pulling her to her feet.

My cock slips out of her mouth with a wet pop, and she's left breathless, looking at me like she knows exactly what she's doing.

"Did you like that?"

I press my hand between her thighs, rubbing her through her panties, feeling the heat and wetness that's already soaked through. She gasps, biting her lip as I touch her.

"It was fucking amazing," I murmur into her ear. "I wanted to watch you drink every last drop of me."

"Then why didn't you let me?" she asks, her breath hitching as I rub her harder.

"Because I want more."

With that, I turn her around, pushing her forward until she's bent over, hands braced against the edge of the fountain. Her ass is right in front of me, perfect, begging for my hands. I tug her panties down slowly, savoring the way they slide over her skin, exposing herself to me. My fingers trace the curve of her hips, and I take a moment to admire her—every inch, bare and trembling—ready for me.

Part of me thinks I should go easy on her. After everything she's been through tonight, coming so close to losing her life. But then she grinds her ass back against me, desperate, needy, and I know she wants this as much as I do. Maybe even more.

I tease her, sliding my head against her soaked pussy, rubbing it just enough to make her squirm. She moans, breathless, desperate.

"Please," she begs, her hips pushing back against me, trying to take what I haven't given her yet.

"Tell me what you need."

"I need you inside me. I'm begging you."

I push into her, slipping inside with one hard thrust. She's soaking wet and tight, welcoming my cock with a firm squeeze.

I drive myself deeper, and it feels perfect, like she was made for me. Every inch of her clenches around me, taking me in. Her back arches, her hands gripping the fountain tight, and I know she's mine—completely.

I thrust hard and deep, her moans mingling with the soft bubbling of the fountain. She's loud, raw, and I fucking love it. I reach forward, slipping her bra down and grabbing her tits, her nipples hard beneath my fingers as I rub and pinch them. She gasps, pushing back against me, and I can tell she's close—so damn close.

My hands move to her ass, squeezing her firm cheeks before I swat her hard enough to leave a faint handprint. She yelps then moans, her body craving more.

"You're mine," I growl, my voice rough and possessive. "I'm going to make you come so hard."

"Please," she begs as she pushes back against me, meeting each of my thrusts with more need, more urgency.

I plunge into her faster, deeper, and her whole body starts to tremble. I feel her tightening around my cock, her walls clenching hard, her legs shaking as the orgasm hits her.

She cries out, her pussy pulsing around me, soaking me as she comes, squeezing me so tight it's like she's pulling me deeper with every wave of pleasure that crashes through her.

She's coming completely undone, falling apart on my cock, and I can feel every damn bit of it.

I turn her around, her legs still trembling, barely able to hold her weight. I kiss her hard, tasting the raw need between us, my tongue claiming hers as our mouths crash together. She's still breathless when I lift her off her feet, carrying her to the grass.

I lay back, looking up at her, and command, "I want you to ride me."

Her lips curve into a sly grin as she straddles me. She takes hold of my cock and starts lowering herself down, her wet heat sheathing me inch by inch.

Fucking hell, it's perfect. I can feel every inch of her as she sinks onto me, tight and warm, her pussy stretching to take me in. Her skin is flushed, her eyes locked on mine as she moves, slow and deliberate.

Her body trembles as she bottoms out. I grab her hips, holding her there, feeling her pulsing around me, and I can't get enough of the way she gives into me with that intoxicating mix of submission and control.

She rides me slowly at first, taking her time, and I enjoy every damn second of it.

I watch as her hips roll in a slow, steady rhythm, grinding down on me. Her breasts bounce with each movement, and I reach up, grabbing them, squeezing just enough to make her moan. She arches her back, her lips parting as she gasps, a soft, breathy sound escaping her throat that drives me wild.

Her hands press against my chest, and she picks up the pace, her thighs trembling as she moves faster. The slick heat of her is incredible, gripping me with every thrust, tight and wet. I move my hands down to her hips, guiding her as she rides me harder, the friction building between us.

Her breaths come quicker, little moans and gasps spilling from her lips, her eyes half-closed in pleasure. She starts to buck her hips harder, grinding down on me with more force, chasing her own release. I can feel her getting closer, her movements more frantic, her pussy clenching tighter around me as she gets lost in it, riding the edge of her climax. I sit up, wrapping my arms around her waist, pulling her against me.

I growl into her ear, "Come for me. I want to feel you fall apart on my cock. Do it now."

She gasps, her whole body tightening around me, and then it hits—she comes hard, her pussy gripping me like a vice, squeezing me with every pulse. I lose myself in her, my own release slamming through me at the same time. It's like every nerve in my body is on fire, every muscle tense as I drive up into her, filling her as she shudders and shakes in my arms.

She cries out, her nails digging into my shoulders, her body trembling against mine as she rides out the waves of her orgasm.

Her hips slow as we both catch our breath. She rests her head on my shoulder, her body limp against mine. I hold her there, still deep inside her, feeling her heartbeat slowly return to normal.

For a moment, I'm struck by how this connection feels, like we've crossed a line we can't come back from.

Whatever it is, it's something I didn't expect.

CHAPTER 15

AMELIA

"I need answers."

We're back in the house, in bed, adrenaline still buzzing in my veins, and I'm trying to figure out what the fuck just happened.

How did I go from fearing for my life to this?

I glance over at him, taking in the sight of his body, sculpted like he was born in a gym, all hard lines and muscle. My mind flashes back to earlier—how calm and collected he was during the home invasion. The man killed someone, and yet he's acting as if nothing happened.

Who *does* that? And why am I not running for the hills right now?

He turns his head, eyes catching mine. "What kind of answers are you looking for?"

"You know what kind."

He nods, ready to drop the real details now, and sits up. I do the same, turning and putting a little space between us so that I can face him directly. After everything he's already told me, I'm bracing for some next-level shit. I now know that he was in the Bratva, the Russian Mafia. But whatever he's about to say next feels even heavier.

He takes a deep breath. "My family wasn't just involved with the Bratva. We ran it. My father and grandfather were leaders. I was born into it. I was supposed to succeed them, to run it one day."

I blink, trying to wrap my head around what he's telling me.

"I hated it," he goes on. "The control, the way they made choices for me. So, I bailed. Got out as soon as I could."

"That couldn't have been easy," I say softly.

"No. It wasn't. My parents, my grandparents—they're all dead," he says, his voice flat. "I don't have any family left in the U.S. anymore."

I chew my lip, trying to process it all. "So, you left, just like that?"

He laughs, though it holds no humor. "Not quite. It was more complicated than that. But I've had nearly two years of relative peace. I haven't had to face my past—until tonight."

"How long do you think I'll need to stay here? How long until it's safe for me to go back to my house?"

Melor's phone buzzes. He glances at it, his jaw tightening. "Hopefully not for too long," he says as he gets up and pulls on his clothes.

While he buttons his shirt, he glances back at me. "Stay here. Don't come down until I call for you."

And just like that, he's out the door, leaving me alone, brain still reeling from the chaos of the last few hours. I lean back against the pillows and stare up at the ceiling, still trying to process everything.

No way in hell am I sitting around like some damsel in distress. The second Melor's out the door, I spring out of bed, grabbing my panties off the floor and yanking them on. I rummage through his dresser, finding an oversized shirt and tossing it on. The scent of him hits me, musky and woodsy, and I'm briefly distracted, inhaling deeply before snapping myself out of it.

I hurry to the window that overlooks the front of the house. My eyes widen as I spot three men heading up the steps, each carrying large duffel bags. *The cleaners.* Great. I'm officially part of a mob screenplay.

As I pull on my jeans, flashes of TV crime shows flood my mind and my stomach twists. They are literally cleaning up a murder scene on the floor below me.

I feel a wave of nausea hit me, and for a second, I think I'm going to hurl. The reality of what I'm mixed up in is a whole lot messier than I thought. This isn't just some mysterious hot guy with a dangerous past. This is *real*. And I'm stuck right in the middle of it, with the scent of him still clinging to my skin.

Panic hits me like a freight train.

I crack open the door and listen, the sound of my heart pounding in my ears overshadowing what's happening downstairs. I hear voices coming from the kitchen and then there's a grunt, then a loud thud, like something heavy hitting the floor. After that, laughter.

I freeze, horrified. They're *laughing*? These guys are cleaning up a murder, and they're laughing like it's just another day on the job?

My breath catches in my throat. Is Melor laughing with them? It's hard to tell.

I lean farther out the door, straining to hear his voice. My mind's racing, jumping between the image of him calmly killing that guy earlier and the idea of him now chilling—and laughing—with these psychopaths.

I seriously need to get the fuck out of here. No more standing around like an idiot, hoping things just magically work out. I step back into the bedroom and look for my shoes. I slip them on before grabbing my phone and shoving it in the back pocket of my jeans.

I tiptoe down the hall, my nerves on edge, every little creak of the floor making me want to crawl out of my skin. As I sneak toward the stairs, I freeze, hearing a voice getting louder. My stomach drops.

I flatten myself against the wall, heart hammering in my chest, watching the kitchen with absolute dread. I hold completely still like a deer caught in the headlights. I wait, but no one comes out. The voices stay where they are, and I slowly exhale.

So far, so good. Now, I just need to make it to the front door without getting caught.

I creep to the corner and peek around, trying to get a glimpse into the kitchen. Sure enough, there's a team at work—three rough-looking dudes speaking rapid-fire Russian, with black beanies pulled low, tattoos snaking up their necks and across their hands.

They move with a calm efficiency; clearly, they've done this before. One guy's unrolling a tarp on the floor and smoothing it out like he's prepping for an art project. Another's reaching into an open duffel bag, and I catch a glimpse of a hacksaw and some industrial-strength gloves inside.

The lifeless body still lies on the kitchen floor, blood pooled around the head like something straight out of a horror movie. My eyes dart to Melor, who's standing nearby, not laughing with them, but also not looking one bit fazed. Just... cold.

I tear my eyes away before allowing myself to get sucked into this morbid trainwreck.

Focus, Amelia.

This is not the time to play detective.

I hurry to the front door, thankful that it's been left open a crack, and slip through. The cool night air hits my face, and I can finally breathe again.

I sprint across the street, my heart feeling like it's about to explode. Once I reach my house, I slam the door behind me, and collapse onto the couch. The tears hit hard and fast. The reality of all that happened tonight hits me full force, and I'm completely overwhelmed, my emotions all over the place.

I shake my head in an attempt to shove the feelings down deep. I can't go there, not now.

I rush to the kitchen and pour myself a much-needed glass of wine. I slug it back in one go, the burn settling my nerves just a bit. Now it's time to think.

Yes, the man that got away knows where I live. But I doubt he will actually be coming back for me. I'm just a side quest. A character with no real stake in the game. I'll be fine if I just lay low for a bit.

I grab a duffel and start tossing clothes in. I'll head to Claire's, hide out for a few days, and figure it all out from there. It wouldn't make sense for anyone to come after me, to involve more people.

To leave a longer trail of bodies.

CHAPTER 16

MELOR

"This one's a bleeder," one of the guys mutters in thickly accented English, chuckling as he pulls the tarp tightly around the body. "My wife will think I've been butchering pigs again."

They laugh, low and grim, the kind of dark humor only men like them can understand. They've done this so many times, it's practically routine. I stay quiet, not joining in their macabre candor.

I have no problem taking a life when I need to, but I've seen men get comfortable with it. *Too* comfortable. It changes you, twisting something inside until killing becomes just another routine task. I swore long ago never to allow myself to get to that point.

"I could do this in my sleep," another cleaner mutters as he zips up his duffel bag. I glance at him but don't respond. I'm not interested in small talk, especially not about this. My phone chimes, and I pull it out, glancing at the screen. The notification shows footage from the front door camera. It's Amelia, slipping out, and hurrying across the street.

Of course.

I sigh, sliding the phone back into my pocket. "I've got a problem I need to handle," I tell the cleanup crew. "Keep things moving here. I'll be right back."

One of them raises an eyebrow. "Need us to handle that problem for you, boss?"

I shake my head, already heading for the door. "No. This one's mine."

Amelia's about to learn that no matter how fast she runs, she's in too deep to escape now.

It's late, close to midnight. I walk up to the porch, scanning the quiet, dim street.

I test the handle. It's locked, but that doesn't stop me. With a quiet, practiced motion, the soft click of the lock gives way. I push the door open, stepping inside without a sound.

She gasps, her eyes going wide as soon as she sees me standing there. I stroll in, calm and controlled, effortlessly slipping the duffel bag from her shoulder, and setting it on the floor beside her.

"What do you think you're doing?" I ask.

She crosses her arms, defiant. "If I'm in danger, I'm getting out of Dodge. You can let me know when the coast is clear."

Despite the situation, I feel a spark of admiration. She's tough, insistent on standing her ground, and I like that.

She's also scared—I can see it in the way her breath catches, the hesitance in her stance—but she's not crumbling.

"You don't need to run away," I say, stepping closer. "The only way to guarantee your safety is if you stay with me."

Her expression softens, and she bristles, pulling back slightly. "I can't just put my life on hold, Melor. I have a job, friends, a business to run."

I stare at her for a long moment, letting her words hang between us. She doesn't get it yet. She thinks she can outrun this. I take another step forward, my eyes locked on hers.

"You don't have any other options," I say, my voice cold and final. "If you want to live, you'll come with me."

Her eyes narrow. "Can't you just keep an eye on me from across the street? You know, without all the drama?"

I let out a sharp laugh, causing her to flinch. "You have no security cameras, and I was able to pick the lock on your front door in under twenty seconds. I wouldn't be able to get to you in time if they come for you here.

"My place is the only option. It's locked down and reinforced. Secure as it gets. And I'm the best protection you're going to find, whether you like it or not."

She glares at me defiantly. "How can you say that? Those guys were able to get into your place, so maybe it isn't as secure as you seem to think it is."

I nod, granting her that concession. "That was a one-time error. It will not happen again."

She opens her mouth to speak but I cut her off. "You have no idea what you're up against. The men who want me dead? They'll use *you* to get to me. And they won't just kill you, Amelia. They'll do things to you that you can't even imagine. You think you're scared now? You have no clue what terror awaits you if you don't listen to me."

Her face pales slightly, and I press further. "I can keep you safe. It won't be for long; you can work on your book. Hell, I'll set up a whole space for you, make sure you're comfortable. You can even bake in my kitchen if you want."

She's silent for a moment, staring at me like she's weighing her options. But her only option is me.

She looks at me, frowning. "How long are we talking about?"

"Maybe a couple of weeks. Just until things cool down."

She balks, shaking her head. "I need to be at the bakery every day, Melor. I have to do deposits, inventory, bake, keep things running. I can't just leave Claire in a lurch like that. She's about to have a baby."

I feel my jaw tighten. "You'll have to tell Claire you have a family emergency. That's the easiest way."

Her eyes flash, and she crosses her arms. "I don't have any family. Claire's the closest thing to family I've got. I'm not about to lie to my best friend like that."

That doesn't sit well with me. "Anybody that you tell the truth to about what's going on will be in danger. This isn't a game, Amelia. If you talk, and the wrong people find out, it won't just be your life on the line."

Her chin tilts up disobediently. "I'll tell her the truth, but I'll make sure she keeps it a secret. Claire wouldn't say a word if she knew what was really going on. She deserves to know. I will not keep her in the dark."

I stare at her, frustration building. I don't like this. One person knowing is one too many. But she's not budging, and something about the way she's standing there, arms crossed like she's already made her decision, tells me I won't win this fight easily.

"Fine," I say, my voice edged with warning. "But if you're going to tell her, you better make damn sure she doesn't tell *anyone* else. No slipups."

She sighs reluctantly. "Okay," she mutters.

A wave of relief washes over me. "You made the right call."

"I need to pack more stuff," she says, already moving toward the bedroom.

"Go ahead."

As she disappears into the other room, something unfamiliar settles over me. I'm glad she's coming back, not just for the security aspect, though knowing she'll be safe, like she's locked in a bank vault and untouchable, is a relief.

But there's more to it than that. I catch myself thinking about what it'll be like to have her there, in my space. The idea of getting to know her, spending time with her— it shouldn't thrill me, but it does. I barely know this woman, yet the thought of her being close to me feels right.

Before I can think too much about it, she reappears, lugging two big bags with her. I step forward, grabbing them with one hand and reaching out with the other.

"Time to go."

She looks at me for a moment, then takes my hand without a word.

CHAPTER 17

AMELIA

Every noise in this damn house sounds like someone creeping up to get me.

I'm in the guest bedroom, lying on my back and staring up at the ceiling, every creak and gust of wind sounds like it's my final warning.

The events of tonight are playing on repeat in my head like some twisted true crime episode I can't turn off.

I'm scared.

Are there men out there right now looking for me? Stalking the streets, waiting for the perfect moment to swoop in and do who knows what? Are they watching my house? The thought makes my skin crawl, and no matter how many times I tell myself that Melor's house is a fortress, that I'm safe here, I can't shake the anxiety that is gnawing away at me.

I roll over, pulling the covers tightly around me, but sleep will not come. Not tonight. Not with all this uncertainty swirling around in my head.

I can't just lie here, so I get up and make my way over to one of the windows that overlooks Melor's garden, where rows of perfectly manicured bushes, flowers that probably cost more than my mortgage, and soft lights cast a ghostly glow over everything.

The second my eyes land on the garden, my mind betrays me. I flash back to the two of us out there earlier, and damn, it hits me like a truck. The way I'd ridden him hard, the rush of power, the heat between us. I close my eyes, letting myself slip back into that moment for just a second, how good it felt, how wild it was.

Before I can get too carried away, I shake my head, snapping back to reality. Seriously, what the hell is wrong with me? Here I am, my life literally on the line, dragged into some insane world I don't understand, and all I can think about is sex?

I turn back to the room, the silver moonlight spilling across the floor. It's quiet, too quiet, and all I can hear are my own thoughts spiraling. I'm starting to get it—my life is about to change forever. I can feel it hanging in the air, but it still hasn't fully sunk in. Maybe it hasn't hit me yet because it's just too unreal, like I'm living in someone else's twisted fantasy.

My thoughts turn to Claire and the bakery. I can't just disappear and leave her to run everything by herself. She's seven months pregnant and the holidays are rapidly approaching. I will not abandon her or our dream.

Out of nowhere, fatigue slams into me. I barely make it back to the bed and collapse onto it, too tired to even pull the covers up.

Just like that, sleep takes over.

～

I wake up feeling like no time has passed.

One second, I'm out cold, and the next, my eyes are wide open, the dim morning light filtering in through the tinted windows. It's quiet, calm, almost cave-like. I check my phone. It's nearly 9 a.m., and my stomach growls like it hasn't been fed in days. I'm starving.

I drag myself out of bed, smoothing down the oversized shirt I slept in, and make my way downstairs. The smell of food cooking hits me before I even reach the kitchen, and it's heavenly. Bacon, eggs, sausage—the works. My mouth is watering.

Melor's standing at the stove, cooking like it's just another Sunday morning, wearing a simple gray t-shirt that hugs his chest and arms, and dark jeans that grip his perfect ass.

He glances over his shoulder as I step into the kitchen. That crooked smile of his makes an appearance, and I feel it right in my chest.

"Morning," he says, his voice chipper like we didn't just go through hell a few hours ago.

I blink, momentarily thrown off by how normal this feels, standing here in his house, my stomach rumbling, while the most dangerous man I've ever met cooks me breakfast.

I slide into one of the bar chairs, still feeling like I'm in some kind of dream.

"How are you feeling?" he asks as he places a steaming mug of coffee in front of me.

I say nothing at first, my eyes drifting to the spot where the body had been last night. The floor's spotless, like it never even happened. No blood, no evidence of the horror of just a few hours ago. But I can still feel the weird energy buzzing through the room, reminding me that something dark went down right here.

I sniff, picking up the faint scent of cleaner beneath the mouthwatering smell of bacon and eggs. My stomach churns, caught between hunger and nausea.

Melor catches me looking and walks over, blocking my view with his body. He takes my hand in his, squeezing it gently, and then, without a word, he lifts it to his lips and kisses the back of it.

"You're safe," he promises.

I stare at him, relishing the warmth of his touch, but I'm not sure I can believe him, not after what I've seen.

"It's so surreal. There was a dead guy here and now we're preparing to have breakfast."

He nods in understanding. "It's a shock to the system the first time you see something like that."

Melor squeezes my hand one more time as he gives me that intense look of his before heading back to the stove to finish up breakfast. He sets it in front of me—crispy bacon, perfectly cooked eggs, sausage, and a slice of toast.

He smirks. "Not exactly the fancy baked goods you're used to, but I like to keep things protein heavy."

I snicker, grabbing a fork. "Yeah, not all of us are out here building muscle 24/7, Captain Gains."

He chuckles, and I dig in, realizing I'm way hungrier than I thought. The food tastes as good as it smells, and I devour it like I haven't eaten in days.

As I shovel in another bite, Melor leans against the counter, arms crossed. "You know," he says casually, "you're welcome to sleep in my bed. You don't have to use the guest room if you don't want to."

I pause mid-chew, then swallow slowly, glancing up at him. The way he says it isn't pushy, but there's definitely a vibe there. I take a breath, wiping my mouth.

"Thanks, but, uh... I think I'll stick to the guest room for now."

He doesn't argue. "That's fine, though I hope you'll change your mind in the next few days. In fact, I'm going to be doing my best to make sure that happens."

I can't help but smile a little. "We'll see," I reply, amused by how sweet that sounded coming from a guy like him.

I shift in my seat, loving the way Melor is all insistent but still respectful of my boundaries. It's a delicate balance, and I've got to admit, he's nailing it.

He glances over at me. "Did you sleep well?"

"Yeah," I say, thinking back to how hard I crashed. "Considering." I poke at the last bit of sausage on my plate. "I can't remember the last time I slept past 8 a.m. Baker's hours start at the crack of dawn."

He gives me a small smile. "Sounds rough."

"Brutal," I say with a dramatic eye roll. "But, yeah, this is the first time in forever I've slept this late."

I sit back, feeling a little more awake, when it suddenly hits me—I need to call Claire. I open my mouth to bring it up, but before I can even get the words out, Melor says, "You should call her."

Damn, how does he read my mind like that?

I blink, surprised. "Yeah, I really should."

"Finish your breakfast first. Get your bearings. You've been through a lot."

I again glance over at the spot where the body was, my eyes lingering on the clean floor. "What's going to happen to him?"

Melor smirks a little like he's amused. "Whatever was going to happen already happened."

"No, I mean the body. What are those guys going to do with it?"

His expression shifts, a little more serious now, but still casual. "You don't need to worry about that, Amelia."

I lean forward, not letting it go. "No. I'm a part of this now, right? Your world? I want to know how it works. I'm not going to be some clueless girl sitting in the dark while all this goes down around me."

He studies me for a second then nods like he respects the pushback.

"Alright," he says, leaning against the counter again. "There are a few ways they handle something like this. Sometimes they'll dump the body somewhere remote, burn it, and make sure there's nothing left to identify. Other times, they'll bury it deep—far enough out of sight that no one stumbles on it. And then there's the more creative approaches: acid, industrial tools, weighing it down and dropping it in water."

I swallow, feeling the weight of every option he's laid out, each one more horrifying than the last. "Okay, then. Good to know."

"These men are pros," Melor continues. "They've probably got a place where they dissolve the body down to nothing, leaving no trace behind."

I flinch at the thought of a person just vanishing like that, erased from existence.

He catches my reaction, his brow knitting slightly. "Sorry," he says, a little softer. "Didn't mean to be so direct."

"No, that's what I wanted," I reply quickly. I asked for the truth, and now I've got it. I glance down at my empty plate and mutter, "Glad I ate first, though."

He chuckles, but it seems forced. "I'm going to do my best to make sure you never see anything like that again. I promise you."

I look up at him, appreciating the sentiment, but a part of me wonders if he can really pull that off. No amount of promises can wipe that away. Still, I nod and offer a small, "Thanks."

But my mind doesn't stay on the violence for long; it drifts right back to Claire. What the hell am I going to tell her? *Hey, bestie, don't freak out, but Mr. Sexy Accountant turned out to be a Russian mobster who killed a dude after we had sex last night. I'm hiding out with him, so you need to cover my shifts, k?*

Melor studies me for a second. "What's on your mind?"

"Claire," I admit. "I have no idea how I'm going to explain this to her without sounding like a complete maniac."

He nods, thinking for a moment, then his face brightens with an idea. "Tell her I invited you on a trip for Thanksgiving. something spontaneous, and you said yes."

I raise an eyebrow. "She'd never buy it. She's known me since I was a kid. Besides, she knows I'd never leave her during our busiest time of the year for some dude I just met. No offense."

He chuckles, making that low, rumbling sound that gets under my skin in all the right ways. "None taken."

I think for another minute, then snap my fingers. "I think I've got an idea that would work. There's a pastry class in LA I've been dying to take but they never have openings. I can tell her I got in on a last-minute cancellation."

"Sounds reasonable," Melor agrees.

I slip off the stool and call Claire, the lie tasting bitter on my tongue, especially as her excitement grows. "Oh my God, that's awesome Am! You've been wanting to do this for a long time. It'll help the business for sure."

Great. I'm going to have to figure out a way to actually step up my skills. "I know it's coming at the worst time," I say apologetically.

"Nonsense. I'll call Susie. She can cover for as long as we need her."

"You're the best, Claire," I tell her, the guilt nearly eating me alive.

"Yeah, I know," she giggles. "Now go learn some awesome shit."

We hang up and I walk back into the kitchen, sighing as I put my phone on the counter.

"Everything okay?" Melor asks.

"Yeah. One of our friends from culinary school is going to help out while I'm gone. She helps us from time to time. I just feel so awful lying to my best friend."

"It's for the best," Melor reminds me. "It protects Claire and you to keep her in the dark."

I nod, knowing he's right but hate every second of it.

Melor's eyes flicker with something like another idea sparking. "Come with me," he says, holding out his hand. "There's something I want to show you."

CHAPTER 18

AMELIA

He leads me up the stairs, all the way to the top floor of the house.

He stops in front of a door at the end of the hall and turns to me with a small smile. "I have a space for you, for your writing."

My mouth drops as he opens the door, revealing a tower room I didn't even know existed. I step inside and wow—the room is adorable, cozy but not cramped, with big windows that give a stunning view of the city below. Light floods into the space, bouncing off the soft-colored walls and wooden floors. It's like this hidden magical hideaway all for me.

I gasp, stepping further inside. "Holy shit. This is gorgeous."

Melor chuckles softly behind me. "I figured if you're going to be stuck here for a while, you might as well have a place where you can work. Write your book. Think of it as your own little private corner of the house."

The room is completely devoid of furniture, and I raise an eyebrow, glancing back at Melor.

"You can spend the day picking out whatever you want," he says "We can't leave the house, obviously, but you can shop online and order what you like. It'll be here by tomorrow."

I blink. Did this man just give me a blank check to decorate my own dream room? "You're telling me I can just... go wild?"

He nods, a small smile tugging at his lips. "I want you to have a space that's yours. A place where you can tap into your creative spirit. Have at it and order what you like, make it feel like home."

My heart does a weird little flutter at that. I glance around the room, already picturing what I could do with it. "Can I grab some stuff from my house, too?"

"Anything you want, if it helps you feel more comfortable."

I walk over to the windows, and I'm stunned again when I catch sight of the view of the city stretches all the way to the bay. It's so breathtaking it makes me gasp.

"Thanks," I murmur.

"I'll be around if you need anything."

Once he leaves, I turn back to the window and stare out at the city below.

This nightmare is turning into a dream.

～

Three weeks later...

I stand in the middle of the grand chamber, glaring at the luxurious "prison" I've been forced into.

The stone walls are cold, but the bed is fit for a queen—high posts, velvet curtains wrapping around a luxurious cloud-like mattress covered in embroidered pillows and handmade quilts. A fire crackles in the hearth. I suppose it's all by design, to make me feel better about being locked away here.

I march over to the window, pulling back the heavy drapes. Of course, I'm in the highest tower. The view is stunning—rolling hills, the forest stretching as far as the eye can see, a river running right through the middle of it all.

Despite its beauty, it's nothing more than a reminder of how far away I am from freedom.

I glance down at the dress they've squeezed me into—a ridiculous, over-the-top gown that's more gold thread than actual fabric—beautiful proof that I'm just a shiny piece in someone's game.

I know why I'm here. My family got me tangled up in their political web, trying to curry favor with the duke. I've never even met the man, yet here I am, stuck in his tower like some prized fairy-tale princess.

I grip the edge of the windowsill, staring out at the horizon. What I wouldn't give to be able to run out there, to feel the wind in my hair, the earth under my feet.

To be free.

Just as I'm about to start planning my great escape, the door creaks open behind me.

I whip around, gasping at the sight of who it is.

The duke is tall and broad-shouldered, both refined and dangerous at the same time. His salt-and-pepper hair is cropped short, and his neatly trimmed beard gives him a sexy vibe—like a brilliant professor who's secretly plotting your downfall.

His clothes are perfectly tailored—a dark, high-collared coat with silver buttons that gleam in the firelight, slacks that cling to his thick, muscular legs, and boots polished to a shine. Every inch of him screams power.

But it's his eyes that give me the greatest pause. Dark and intense, sharp enough to cut through steel.

I've heard the stories; everyone has. The duke is ruthless, to say the least. His reputation on the battlefield is legendary—it's been said he destroys his enemies without hesitation or mercy.

And then there are the whispers about his insatiable thirst for women.

He steps in, closing the door behind him, his gaze locking onto mine.

"Are you finding the accommodations to your liking, my lady?"

"They're fine," I say, keeping my voice steady though my heart is racing. "But I want to leave."

He laughs and takes a step closer, then another. He's right in front of me now, close enough to feel the heat radiating off him. "You're not going anywhere," he says, voice low and dangerous. "Not until I get what I want."

My breath catches. "And what is it you want?"

He's mere inches away now, towering over me, his presence nearly suffocating. He smirks. "Isn't it obvious?" His eyes scan me up and down, dark, and hungry. "I want you."

I want to resist him; I should resist him. But my body betrays me—I'm already soaking through my underthings, every part of me tingling.

His lips curl into a wicked grin. "I've wanted you from the moment I saw you," he says, his voice a low, dangerous rumble. "And now, you're all mine."

I swallow hard, trying to hold onto some shred of defiance. "You'll never have me," I manage to say, my voice hesitant and weak.

He grins as he sweeps his hand around the lavish room. "Can't you see? You're already mine. Look around. I already have you."

I shake my head, trying to ignore the pounding in my chest. "No. I'll resist you every step of the way."

"Resist me?" he chuckles, and I can feel his breath on my skin. "I can tell that's not what you want."

My cheeks flush hot, and I tilt my chin up, challenging him. "Prove it."

His eyes darken, a flicker of raw hunger crossing his face. And then, without warning, he grabs me, pulling me hard against his chest, crashing his lips into mine. The kiss is rough, demanding, his grip growing firmer as he takes what he wants. My knees weaken, my resolve crumbling beneath his intensity.

I pull away, breathless, my mind a blur, my body on fire. I'm so aroused I can barely think straight.

"I can't feel this way about you," I stammer, my heart racing. "You're a blackguard, a killer."

He grins, that dangerous smirk that both terrifies and thrills me. "That's exactly what turns you on, isn't it?"

I'm speechless. No man has ever dared to speak to me like this, especially not a lady of my station. His words shock me to my core, leaving me momentarily frozen.

Without another word, he moves in and effortlessly scoops me up, cradling me against his chest as he strides toward the bed. My pulse quickens even more, my breathing shallow.

"What are you going to do?"

His eyes gleam with dark intent as he lays me down on the bed, his body hovering over mine. "I'm going to do what you've been fantasizing about since we met," he growls, his voice thick with desire.

I want to protest, to deny it, but I can't. He's got me pegged, reading my every thought like an open book. Before I can find the words to argue, his hands are on me, sliding up my dress, moving along the curve of my thigh, sending shivers up my spine.

When his hand reaches my slip, my body arches against him, a moan slipping from my lips. I've never been touched like this before, and every inch of me is aching for more.

His fingers tease my womanhood, exploring me in a way no one ever has. My body becomes alight with want, a frenzy of need building inside me, and I can see the dark satisfaction in his eyes as he watches me come undone beneath his touch. He loves the control he has over me.

"What do you want?" he growls, his voice low and thick with dominance.

I can't help it; the words slip from my lips before I can stop them.

"I want more. More of this. More of you."

His smirk widens, and he climbs on top of me, his weight pressing me into the bed as he grinds his manhood against me. The heat between us is unbearable, and my hands move on their own, undoing the front of his pants. The moment his hardness leaps into my hand, I moan, my body trembling with anticipation. I guide him to my entrance, ready for him to take me completely.

He begins to slide in, and—

CLANG!

A loud crash jolts me back to reality.

A damn garbage truck slams its way down the street below. I blink, shaking my head, and realize I'm in my writing room, fully dressed, laptop open in front of me. I stare down at the page, the scene I'd been crafting vivid and intense, so real I'd forgotten where I was for a moment.

"Jesus," I mutter to myself. Talk about being in the zone.

I stand up and stretch, feeling the satisfying pop in my back. A smile spreads across my face as I glance at my laptop. Holy shit, I've written more in the last few weeks since moving in than I have all year. I lean back in my chair, grinning.

"Thanks for the inspo," I mutter to myself, thinking of the handsome, brooding man I'm currently living with. Melor, the muse behind my fictional Duke Allsbrook—a deadly, sexy force of nature.

I take a moment to look around my writing room. It's perfect. There's greenery everywhere, potted plants on the windowsill, ivy trailing down the bookshelves that are packed with every writing guide I need. The napping couch has been a lifesaver, allowing me to regroup and reset whenever I need to.

But honestly, the real game-changer has been Melor. He's made sure I don't want for anything. Whether it's coffee, food, a new writing guide or notebook, it just magically appears. It's like having a personal assistant that looks like he just stepped out of a *GQ* spread. Oh, and is also a trained killer.

I laugh to myself. If I could only forget that pesky little detail about my life being in constant danger, this setup would be downright dreamy.

As I make my way to the second floor, I catch myself thinking about the last few weeks. It's been a weird mix of normal and completely surreal. For instance, last night I made dinner for Melor. Nothing fancy, just baked chicken and roasted potatoes, but he seemed to love it. It felt so... domestic.

After dinner we watched the movie *Crazy, Stupid, Love,* laughing at the ridiculousness of Ryan Gosling trying to coach Steve Carell into being a ladies' man. It actually felt like we were in a real relationship, not just two people hiding out, especially seeing as we had sex afterward.

I shiver at the memory, smiling to myself as I save my work and close my laptop. There was a moment last night when he was on top of me, his hand sliding between my thighs, his fingers doing that thing that makes me lose my mind. He kept a slow, torturous pace, whispering in my ear, telling me how he loved the way I was falling apart beneath him.

And then, just when I couldn't take it anymore, he moved faster, and I came so hard I swear I saw stars.

It's been easy at times to forget the danger lurking outside these walls, the reason I'm even here.

My phone buzzes, yanking me away from my thoughts. It's Claire. I can already feel the excitement in her as I answer.

"Amelia! How's the class going? Tell me everything!"

I bite my lip, scrambling to come up with false details. "Oh, it's amazing," I say, keeping it short and sweet so as not to trip myself up in more lies. "I'm learning a lot."

"I'm so glad you'll be back on Monday. Susie's been great, but I miss my partner in crime."

"I miss you, Claire Bear."

"Well, I'll let you get back to it. But seriously, I can't wait to see you and hear all about your trip."

"Me, too," I force out, trying to match her energy. We say our goodbyes and I step into the kitchen.

I hate lying to her, but if it's what I need to do to keep her safe, I'll do it.

CHAPTER 19

MELOR

"So, are you saying you want me to kill them?" Viktor Mashkov asks.

I pace around the room like a caged tiger, fingers clenched around the phone, trying to figure out how to respond. It would be easy to say yes, to let him handle this. But this time is different. I stop and close my eyes.

"I want to do this myself."

There's a pause, then a dark chuckle. "You were always a stubborn one, Melor."

I smirk, shaking my head. "It's personal, Viktor. You know that." I can hear him shifting on the other end, probably lighting up one of his cigars. "Besides, I'm no longer in the Bratva. I knew when I left if I had to take matters into my own hands, I would."

"Your father raised you right," Viktor grumbles. "But don't forget, I did you a favor releasing you from your obligations. That's not something I offer lightly."

"I haven't forgotten," I say, my voice softening. I owe the old man more than I can ever repay. When he let me walk away from the Bratva, it wasn't just business—it was a personal favor to my father, something he didn't have to do. "You've always treated me like your own. I know that."

Mashkov sighs. "And I think of you as a son, Melor. But understand this—if you need help, I will send it. Even if you refuse."

I smile grimly. "I appreciate that. But this one's mine."

A heavy silence hangs between us before Mashkov speaks again. "Take care of it, then. Don't let it linger."

"I won't."

"Do you have any leads on who it was?"

I run a hand through my hair, staring out the window. "The man said I killed his brother."

"Well, then, that's a start," Mashkov replies.

I grit my teeth. "I've killed many men over the years. How the hell am I supposed to remember a particular one?"

There's a pause on his end before he admits, "That's a good point. I suppose narrowing it down to just one dead brother would be a bit of a challenge for someone like you."

"Yeah, that's an understatement." I lean against the wall, the frustration settling deeper. "There's nothing specific I can remember about any of them. Nothing that stands out."

"Nothing at all? It's not like you to miss details, Melor. At least, it never used to be."

I think back to the encounter, the rush of violence, the adrenaline. Nothing comes to mind. It was just another attempt on my life, faceless, like the others. "Nothing. They're just ghosts in the dark."

Mashkov lets out a long sigh. "Then you're at a dead end."

I nod, even though he can't see me. "Yes, seems that way."

"Be careful, Melor," Mashkov says quietly. "Ghosts can still be dangerous."

A fresh wave of anger surges through me as I recall the night those bastards invaded my home, my sanctuary, and threatened Amelia. The thought of her being dragged into this, into my world, sets my blood on fire.

"So," Mashkov breaks the silence, his voice more curious now. "Tell me about this woman."

I hesitate for a second before giving in. He has the resources to find out anything he wants to know anyway. "She's the owner and operator of a bakery. Tough, sarcastic, but there's a sweetness underneath it all. She's driven, focused—works harder than anyone I know. The kind of woman who doesn't take shit from anyone."

"Ahh," Mashkov says, amused. "A woman with some fire. It's about time you found someone. Your life was getting boring."

I let out a low chuckle despite myself. "You've always said I live like an old man."

"It's true," he replies playfully. "But I'm glad you've found someone who shakes things up a bit. You need that."

The bond between Viktor and me goes beyond boss and soldier. We've shared too much blood, too many secrets for it to be anything less.

"Listen, Melor," he says, voice heavy with the weight of experience. "I know what it's like when scum try to use the people we care about to get to us. There's a particular kind of rage that comes with it."

I clench my jaw, the truth of his words cutting deep. "Part of the reason I chose this life was so that I didn't have anyone close. No one who could be used against me."

Mashkov sighs. "But life, my boy, doesn't always respect your choices."

"You're right," I admit, the frustration gnawing at me. "I'm going to take care of the son of a bitch as soon as I find him."

"Melor," Mashkov says, his tone shifting back to that of the seasoned leader I used to follow. "I can get in touch with my contacts on the West Coast. They have men that can take care of this bastard for you. You don't need to get your hands dirty."

I shake my head, pacing the room again. "Thank you, Viktor, but no."

A long pause on his end, and then a sigh. "You're too much like your father in that way."

I smirk but stay silent. He's not wrong.

"But" Mashkov adds, "at least let me help in some way. Let me send someone. We might be able to sniff him out before he makes another move. Think about it, it's not just you who's in danger here."

I stop pacing, considering his offer. I don't like relying on others, but Mashkov is right—it's foolish not to accept a little help when it's being offered, especially when someone else's life is involved.

"Fine," I relent. "Have someone keep an ear to the ground. See what they can dig up. I want to know the second that fucker surfaces."

Mashkov's voice lightens, clearly glad I'm accepting the help. "Consider it done."

We exchange a few more words before ending the call. As I hang up, I feel the weight of unfinished business settling in. This isn't over. Not by a long shot.

I slip my phone back into my pocket and head downstairs to the kitchen, the scent of simmering stew fills the air. I glance at the oven, where a loaf of bread is baking, the golden crust starting to crackle. Dinner is almost ready.

As I slowly stir the stew, my mind drifts back to the past week. Amelia's been back at work, and while I know she needs her routine, it hasn't exactly been sitting well with me.

I insist on driving her to and from the bakery every day, making it clear that leaving work once she's there isn't an option. It's simply not safe.

She hates it. I can see it in the way her jaw tightens every time I bring it up. She understands the gravity of the situation, but she also craves her freedom, and I've had to take some of that away.

It's been nearly a month since she stumbled into my world, and as unexpectedly enjoyable as it's been having her around, I know it can't last. I'm not built for this, for being this close to someone. And once I find the remaining man who broke in and neutralize the threat, we'll return to our separate lives.

If that's even possible anymore.

Still stirring the stew absentmindedly, my thoughts pull me in two directions. Part of me knows what needs to be done—solve the problem, eliminate the threat, and allow Amelia to go back to her life.

I chose this solitary path because it's simple, controlled, and I have no one to worry about but myself. That's the life I've built, the life that's kept me alive.

But a greater part of me doesn't want to let her go. It gnaws away at me, this unfamiliar pull, this desire to keep her close. Even if she doesn't stay in my home, part of me wants her to stay in my life.

Hell, just hearing her laughter coming from the other room makes me feel things I never thought I could. It opens up something in me I've kept locked away for years.

The logical side of me fights back. This arrangement was supposed to be temporary, a situation to handle and move on from. And yet, I find myself stalling.

It's been quiet the last few weeks. No signs of the assassin, no threats, no suspicious movements. I've been watching her house, the bakery, checking in on her multiple times a day from a distance, making sure everything's still locked down. The silence almost feels unnatural, like the calm before the storm.

I know the assassin hasn't forgotten. He hasn't given up. He's waiting. Biding his time.

And the longer this goes on, the harder it's getting to imagine a life without her in it.

I hear footsteps and look up to see Amelia standing at the entrance to the kitchen. Damn, she looks good.

She's still in her work clothes—a pair of tight, dark jeans that hug her hips just right, and a white T-shirt so thin I can see the outline of her bra underneath. The sight of her makes my pulse quicken and my cock stirs to life at the way she's so effortlessly sexy.

"I couldn't wait any longer," she says, her voice playful. "Dinner smells too good."

I smile, nodding toward the table. "Sit. It's ready."

She comes into the room and takes a seat at the table while I ladle stew into two bowls.

Amelia watches me with those sharp, bright eyes as I pull the loaf of bread out of the oven, its crust crackling in the heat. I cut two thick slices, setting them on plates with a small dish of butter on the side. I can't help but enjoy this small domestic moment, even though my mind's been tangled with conflicting thoughts all day.

She smiles, and for a second it feels like this situation—*us*—is something more than just temporary.

That's because it has to be for her sake. At least that's what I keep telling myself.

After a few bites, Amelia's face lights up. "God, this is amazing, Melor. Your cooking might actually inspire me to try some new things out in the bakery. Maybe I'll add a few soups to the menu." She grins, clearly pleased with the idea.

I smirk, enjoying her reaction. "That could work well, especially in the cooler months. It might help bring in a bigger lunch crowd. How's everything going there, by the way?"

Her expression shifts, just slightly, and I can see her tense up. She shrugs, avoiding my gaze. "It's fine."

I set my spoon down, watching her carefully. "What's wrong?"

She sighs, her shoulders slumping a bit. "It's just hard to relax with, well, you know, everything that's going on."

I've watched her carry this weight for weeks, the constant worry she tries to hide. "I get it. I'll solve this mess soon, and you'll be able to get back to your normal life."

She gives me a small smile, but I can see the tension still lingering. After a beat, she looks at me, a little hesitation in her eyes. "So, Claire has seen you dropping me off and picking me up every day. She's grilling me about you. She wants to have us over for dinner at their place."

I pause, surprised by the proposal. "That sounds like a great idea."

Her entire face lights up with the biggest, brightest smile, and I feel something inside me shift. I lean over the table, catching her lips in a kiss. She melts into it, and her smile widens as I pull away.

"You know, I'm suddenly not so hungry for food anymore."

CHAPTER 20

AMELIA

Melor pounces on me like a damn predator, pulling me up from my chair and lifting me up onto the kitchen bar. The cool surface of the bar sends a shiver up my spine as my bare skin touches it. I let out a surprised laugh as he presses his body against mine, his lips brushing my neck.

"Still covered in flour from work, I see." His hands are already working on the button of my jeans.

I smirk, biting my lip. "I am. And you're about to be covered in it, too."

He grins, slowly tugging my jeans down, just enough to expose me to his touch. His fingers trail over my bare skin, sending a shiver through me as he leans in close. "Mmm," he growls, his voice thick with heat, "I bet your pussy's even sweeter than those treats that you bake."

Oh. My. God.

My breath catches, my entire body lighting up with a sudden, intense heat. I can feel myself getting wetter, the anticipation driving me wild.

His fingers slip under the waistband of my panties, teasing me, rubbing slowly and deliberately. My back arches, and I grip the edge of the bar, trying to keep myself together, but he's driving me insane.

"You like that?" he whispers against my ear, his fingers working their magic. I bite back another moan, my heart racing, the heat between us growing with every second.

His other hand slips under my shirt, fingers sliding beneath the cups of my bra, rubbing my breasts, my nipples hardening under his touch. I let out a shaky breath as his hands work me over, teasing and coaxing every reaction out of me like he knows my body better than I do.

He drops to his knees, his hands gripping my hips, holding me steady. His lips move closer, brushing against the inside of my thighs, teasing me, making me wait for it. I gasp as he kisses higher, his lips soft and firm, my legs trembling in anticipation.

"Melor," I whisper, barely holding it together.

He smirks, and then finally spreads me open, his tongue flicking out to taste me. The sensation sends me reeling—soft, wet, and just the right amount of pressure. He starts slow, licking up and down, teasing the most sensitive part of me with the tip of his tongue before circling it, driving me crazy.

I moan as his tongue works its magic, alternating between soft, torturous licks, and deep, hungry strokes.

It's perfect, and I'm losing control fast.

He slips a finger into me, and a whole new level of pleasure takes hold. His tongue doesn't stop, keeps working my clit with expert precision, while his finger moves inside, curling just right. Every nerve in my body feels like it's on fire, and he knows exactly what he's doing.

I'm so close, right on the edge, and he knows it. He slows down, making me squirm, and then pulls back just enough to speak.

"Ask for it."

My breath catches, and I don't hesitate.

"Please... I need it, right now."

He licks me harder, faster, pushing me over the edge, and I come so hard I can't even think, my entire body trembling, thighs clenching around him. I gasp, the pleasure overwhelming, and he grins as he stands, licking his lips.

"You taste delicious," he growls, his voice rough with hunger. "I could eat that perfect pussy all damn day."

I'm still riding the high, but I'm not done. Not even close. My hand reaches for his pants, undoing them quickly, pulling out his cock. It's long, thick, and hard in my hand, the weight of it heavy in my palm. I admire it for a second, feeling it twitch under my touch, before guiding him closer.

"I need you deep inside me," I say, my voice dripping with need as I place him right at my entrance, teasing him just like he teased me.

I rub myself with the head of his cock, loving how it feels grazing against me. His breath hitches, and I smirk, dragging it out for a moment longer. But then, just when I'm about to keep playing, he takes charge, grabbing his cock by the base and slipping it inside.

I moan instantly, my hips squirming. "More," I beg, "Please, more."

His eyes darken with that familiar hunger, and he doesn't hold back. He gives me what I want, pushing deeper, stretching me out, filling me in that way only he can. I gasp, my nails gripping his arms as he glides all the way in. He feels so good, filling me so perfectly.

"God, you feel so fucking amazing," he groans, his voice low and husky. He starts bucking into me, hard and deep, and I can't help the sounds that escape my lips. The way he moves, how he takes control, is so sexy I can't contain myself.

"You like that?" he murmurs, his words a little sweeter than usual, catching me by surprise. "You're so perfect, wrapped around me."

I gasp, my body trembling under his control, every word sinking in.

"Look at you," he murmurs, his tone softer than usual, but still dripping with that dirty edge. "You're taking me so well. I could stay inside you forever."

My heart races, and I can barely catch my breath. "Melor..." I manage to whisper.

He thrusts harder, gripping my hips. "You're mine. You know that, right? You belong to me."

I moan again, feeling myself falling apart as his words push me even closer.

"That's it, baby," he groans, his voice sweet and sultry. "Come for me. Let go. I want to feel you."

His pace never slows, driving me right to the brink, and I know it's only a matter of seconds before I shatter completely.

I can feel it building, the tension in my body coiling tighter with each of his relentless thrusts. His cock fills me perfectly, hitting all the right spots, but it's not just that—it's the way he's looking at me, like I'm the only thing in his world right now. His grip on my hips tightens, and I can barely hold back.

"You're close, aren't you?" he whispers, his lips brushing my ear, sending shivers down my spine. "I can feel you. Let go, baby. I want to see you come for me."

I can't stop the moan that escapes, my body responding to him in ways I can't control. He shifts, angling himself just right, and suddenly I gasp, my breath coming in short, desperate bursts.

"That's it," he murmurs, slowing down just enough to make it even more intense. His eyes stay locked on mine, and I see something deeper in them. "You're so beautiful like this."

I don't know if it's his words, or the way he's taking his time with me, but I come undone, the pleasure ripping through me in waves. My nails dig into his arms as I cry out, my whole body shaking. Melor watches, a satisfied grin tugging at his lips.

He doesn't stop, though. As I'm catching my breath, he lifts me effortlessly, carrying me over to the couch.

I look up at him, still dazed, but ready for more. He kneels between my legs, his hands sliding up my thighs, his gaze hot and intense.

"Let me make you feel even better," he says softly before leaning down and kissing a slow trail up my inner thigh, taking his time.

Melor's lips work their way up my thigh, his touch sending sparks through my entire body. Every kiss, every brush of his fingers has me melting beneath him. He's so slow, so deliberate, like he's savoring every inch of me. My skin tingles with anticipation, my breath coming faster as he reaches the spot where I need him most.

"God, you drive me crazy," I whisper, barely able to form the words.

He smirks against my skin. "That's the idea."

He shifts, positioning himself between my legs, his cock teasing at my entrance. But instead of rushing, he takes his time, pushing into me so slowly I can feel every inch of him stretching me, filling me again. I gasp, my hands gripping the couch, every nerve in my body tingling.

His eyes lock onto mine, and the intensity in his gaze is like nothing I've ever seen. This isn't just about sex—it's something deeper, more intimate, and it shakes me to my core. "You feel perfect," he murmurs.

The rhythm he sets is steady but deep, each thrust pushing me higher, the heat between us building to a fever pitch. My body starts to tremble, and I know I'm close again.

"Come with me," he growls, his breath ragged.

The mutual climax is unlike anything I've ever felt—intense, raw, and powerful. We fall apart together, my body clenching around him as we come in perfect sync, his deep groans mixing with my cries of immense pleasure.

I can feel the heat of him as he explodes inside me, filling me, and the sensation sends aftershocks rippling through my entire body. It's an overwhelming mix of pleasure and connection that leaves me completely undone.

My breath is ragged, matching his, our bodies pressed together, both of us spent but still riding that high.

When it's over, he leans down and kisses me hard, like he can't get enough. I kiss him back and pull him closer before we finally collapse on the couch. I curl up against his chest and as his arm wraps around me, I realize just how safe I feel with him, how much I'm at peace. For a few perfect moments, I forget all about the danger lurking outside these walls. Right now, all I feel is happy.

"I'm sort of excited to show you off at Claire's."

"I'm not exactly a prize," he says with a light laugh.

"You are, though," I tell him, and watch as he shifts somewhat uncomfortably.

And just like that, the spell is broken.

CHAPTER 21

AMELIA

"I'm telling you, Claire's gonna flip over these cinnamon rolls,"

I'm holding Melor's hand as he helps me out of his car across the street from the bakery. The air's chilly, our breath visible in little puffs. Christmas decorations everywhere are making the city glow. For a moment, it feels weirdly normal, like we're just a regular couple enjoying a holiday stroll.

But then I accidentally bump into him, and my elbow hits something hard under his coat. Oh. Right. The gun.

Because we're not normal.

Not even close.

"You good?" Melor looks down at me, his voice calm but always alert.

"Yeah," I say, forcing a smile. "Just thinking about Christmas. I've never experienced a white one in person. That would be kind of cool."

He smirks, clearly not fooled by my little dodge. "White Christmases are beautiful," he says, his tone soft. "Especially the ones in Moscow."

I can feel him studying me, like he knows there's more I'm not saying. But instead of pushing, he adds, "Maybe you'll see one for yourself someday."

I shrug, playing it off. "Yeah, maybe. I mean, I don't think San Francisco's getting any snow anytime soon, but a girl can dream."

He chuckles, squeezing my hand. I can tell he knows I'm deflecting, but he's smart enough not to push.

We're approaching the stairs to the apartment above the bakery when Melor suddenly asks, "How's the book going?"

I blush immediately. I'm not used to talking about my work. "It's, uh... going good. It's probably not the sort of thing you'd read."

He smirks. "Try me."

I hesitate, then sigh. "It's about a noblewoman who ends up being held captive in the castle of a mysterious, brooding duke."

He lets out a deep laugh, the sound rumbling through him. "Let me guess—little bit of real-life inspiration there?"

I bite my lip, trying not to grin. "Maybe," I say, keeping the fact that some of the more intense scenes were most definitely inspired by him.

Melor's quiet presence beside me is grounding, but on the inside, I'm torn. He gently takes my hand and turns me toward him, leaning in for a kiss. Like always, his kiss melts away my worries, making me all kinds of hot. It's like the rest of the world fades for a second, leaving just us.

I grin up at him after the kiss, feeling lighter. "You always know just what to say, and what not to say."

A voice calls out, "Hey, you two! Get a room!"

I glance up, and there's Claire, leaning out of her window with a huge grin on her face. The building is covered in lovely Christmas lights, garland wrapped around the balconies, giving everything a warm, festive glow. Claire's clearly enjoying her own joke because she waves us off with a laugh.

"I'll be right down!"

Melor grins, squeezing my hand. The door swings open, and there stands Claire, wearing an oversized Christmas sweater stretched tight over her big pregnant belly. She's glowing, and not just from the holiday lights.

"Look at you two, all cozy," Claire teases as she steps aside to let us in.

David's there, looking dapper as always in a button-down shirt and a perfectly fitted sweater. He nods at us, a warm smile on his face.

"Welcome," he says, holding the door open wider for us to step inside.

Upstairs, the apartment is filled with even more Christmas cheer. A big twinkling tree stands in the corner, decked out with ornaments, tinsel, and a sparkly star on top. Garland hangs from the doorways, and holiday candles are flickering on every available surface.

Just as we get settled, their French bulldog, Pancake, comes waddling over to greet us, his little tail wagging excitedly. I crouch down to give him a quick scratch behind the ears before standing back up.

"Claire, David, this is Melor," I say, turning to him. "Melor, this is Claire and David."

Melor shakes David's hand, offering Claire a warm smile. "Nice to meet you both," he says smoothly, reaching into the bag he's carrying. He pulls out a bottle of scotch and hands it to David, who raises his eyebrows in pleasant surprise.

"Good scotch," David says, nodding with approval as he inspects the bottle. "Lagavulin 16-year? Really good scotch."

Melor smirks. "Figured it might be to your taste."

David chuckles clearly impressed. "You figured right."

Not to be outdone, I reach into the bag and pull out the sparkling grape juice for Claire, wiggling it in front of her. "And for you, mom-to-be."

Claire beams. "How thoughtful; thank you."

David gestures toward the spread as we sit at the dining room table. "Tonight, we've got spicy pad Thai, spring rolls, and some coconut sticky rice for dessert."

Claire grins, rubbing her belly. "Cravings have been wild, so Thai it is."

Though the spread looks amazing, a sudden wave of nausea hits me. It's subtle but enough to give me pause. I push it aside—probably just nerves—and refocus on the conversation and food.

Melor turns to David, leaning in. I'm very familiar with what she does, thanks to all the treats Amelia brings over from the bakery." That gets a smile out of Claire. "But David, how about you?"

"I'm a public defender," David replies.

Melor's eyebrows go up, clearly impressed. "That's admirable work. Can't be easy, though, defending people who might not deserve it."

"It's a broken system," David says, taking another bite of his pad Thai. "You see people get steamrolled all the time, especially if they don't have money or connections. My job is to make sure everyone gets a fair shot."

"There are definitely a lot of people who don't, that's for sure. I'm impressed."

David smiles before dropping the inevitable question. "So, Melor, what do you do?"

Without missing a beat, Melor gives that signature, confident smile.

"I own a cybersecurity firm."

David nods approvingly. "Nice. That's got to keep you busy."

As the conversation flows, I start thinking about how, in another time, Melor and David would've been on opposite sides of the law. David, the do-good public defender, and Melor, with his less-than-legal past. It's not hard to imagine, even if Melor is technically retired. Melor would have only the best defense attorneys on his side, but the irony of the two of them sitting together, sharing a meal and discussing their careers... I can't help but snicker to myself.

But then my mind wanders to the bigger question—is Melor really done with his old life?

Deep down I already know the answer. He's not. At any moment, a crazed gunman could kick the door down and remind us of that fact.

Pancake curls up against my leg, his warm little body pulling me back to the present. I let out a breath I didn't even know I was holding. Claire catches my eye from across the table. "You okay, Am?"

Crap.

I force a smile, trying to play it off. "Yeah, just got carried away thinking about some Christmas ideas for the bakery." It was a total lie, but it's better than admitting I was imagining us getting ambushed.

Claire grins, oblivious. "I can't wait to hear them!"

Melor chimes in. "I love seeing her creative process at work."

I glance over at him, my heart doing that annoying fluttery thing again. I offer a weak smile in return, trying to shake off the lingering anxiety.

Maybe I just need some air. Or a reality check.

I turn my attention to the meal in front of me, realizing I haven't taken a single bite. I'm still feeling a little off, but I figure maybe some food will help. I start with a spring roll, dipping it into the peanut sauce on my plate. It's good, but it settles weirdly in my stomach.

Meanwhile, Melor, David, and Claire are chatting away like they've been besties for years. I should feel like I'm part of it, but I don't. I feel like I'm a million miles away.

Still not feeling quite right, I take a bite of the pad Thai.

Big mistake.

The second I start chewing, a wave of nausea hits me like a freight train.

Shit.

"Excuse me," I mutter, standing up quickly, trying not to look too panicked as I rush off to the bathroom. I barely make it, slamming the door shut behind me as I heave over the toilet.

Afterward, I stand there for a moment, catching my breath, leaning over the sink, and staring at myself in the mirror. My face is pale, my heart's racing, and I'm sweating.

What the hell is going on?

CHAPTER 22

AMELIA

"Am? You okay in there?"

A knock at the door pulls me out of my thoughts.

I let out a sigh. "Yeah, come in."

Claire opens the door, slipping inside and closing it behind her. Her brow is furrowed, worry all over her face. "What's going on? You don't look so hot."

I lean back against the sink, running a hand through my hair. "I don't know. I just got sick out of nowhere."

Claire's lips twitch, and she cracks a joke because that's what she does. "You mean my cooking finally got to you?"

I laugh weakly, shaking my head. "No, it's not that. Normally, your pad Thai is amazing. But tonight, the spices hit me weirdly."

Claire's eyes widen, and before I can even blink, she blurts out, "Are you pregnant?"

My stomach drops, and I suddenly feel like I might need to throw up all over again "What? No, I mean, I don't think so?"

Claire raises an eyebrow, giving me that look. "You *don't think so?*"

Oh God. Now I feel like I'm in a full-on panic.

"There's no way I'm pregnant," I say, crossing my arms like that'll somehow make the statement more believable.

Claire raises an eyebrow, her expression all sass. "No way, huh? You're telling me you're not hitting that hunk of man meat out there on the regular?"

I groan, rolling my eyes. "Okay, fine. Yes, we've been having sex. But I'm on the pill."

"Uh-huh. And how many times did you forget to take it?"

I shift uncomfortably, knowing full well she's got a point. With the chaos of the last few weeks, it's highly possible I might've missed a pill. Or two.

Shit.

"Looks like you might wanna pick up a pregnancy test on your way home."

I stand there, looking at her with what I'm sure is a dumb expression on my face.

Claire quickly pulls out a spare toothbrush and hands it to me with some toothpaste. "Here. Freshen up."

I apply the toothpaste, glancing at her in the mirror. "Was my exit super awkward?"

She shrugs, leaning against the sink. "A little abrupt, sure, but Melor suggested to David they crack open the scotch, so they're thick as thieves now. Trust me, they're fine."

Thick as thieves.

Her words hit me, reminding me of Melor's past and the fact that I'm keeping this massive secret from my best friend. I push the guilt down for now. There are more immediate problems at hand.

I spit and rinse, then plop down on the closed toilet seat, feeling like the weight of everything is finally hitting me. "How could I have been so careless? So stupid?"

Claire sits beside me on the edge of the tub, rubbing my back. "Hey, don't beat yourself up. You don't even know if you are yet. You need to take a test."

I nod, my mind still racing, then Claire's eyes widen like she's just had a lightbulb moment. "Wait, I still have two pregnancy tests left over from when David and I were trying!"

My head snaps up. "You do?"

Claire grins, already heading for the bathroom cabinet. "Yep. So, you're in luck, or, maybe not, depending on how this goes."

I try to wave it off, standing up and moving toward the door. "You know, I don't really need to take it right now."

Claire gives me a deadpan look, arms crossed. "Girl, you're being ridiculous. You need to know if you're pregnant."

She finds a test, handing it over like it's no big deal. "Look, I get that you're nervous," she says, her voice softening, "but it's important you know right away so you can make whatever decision you're going to make."

I already know what I'd do if I'm pregnant. I'm keeping the baby, no question. But what about Melor? He's got enough going on without throwing a kid into the mix.

Claire's eyes narrow. "Hey, just breathe, okay? Don't freak out. It's just a test, and it only takes a few minutes. We'll hang out in the nursery and talk baby stuff while we wait."

My mind is swirling. She knows me so well. She already sees the panic in my eyes and is talking me down before I spiral. I take the test from her hand, knowing that whatever happens next, I'll have to deal with it.

I try to lighten the mood with a joke. "Guess I'll need to ask for some of those baby gifts back... might need them for myself."

Claire laughs, rolling her eyes. "Okay, funny girl, now go pee on that damn thing already."

I smirk, but the nerves are creeping in hard. Claire gives me a quick hug and heads to the nursery, promising to meet me there in a few minutes. With a deep breath, I glance at the test in my hand. Two minutes. That's all it takes to potentially change my life.

I do my business, then sigh heavily as I wash my hands, nerves buzzing in my chest. I tuck the test into my pocket and head down the hallway to the nursery, where Claire's already waiting for me. The second I step in, I'm hit with how adorable the space is. The walls are painted a soft pastel yellow, with cute animal decals scattered across them. There's a white crib in the corner, a rocking chair, a changing table, and shelves filled with tiny baby clothes, books, and stuffed animals.

It's perfect. Realizing I might have a baby of my own soon, emotions slam into me like a tidal wave. Tears fill my eyes before I can stop them.

Claire rushes over, pulling me into a tight hug. She quietly shuts the nursery door to give us some privacy. I lean into her, feeling completely overwhelmed.

"Hey, it's okay," she whispers, rubbing my back. "Having a baby is amazing. Being pregnant is wonderful, and just think—what if our kids become best friends? Or grow up and fall in love? That would be a full-circle moment."

I choke out a small laugh through my tears. "It's not just that, Claire. It's... *everything*."

She pulls back a little, frowning. "What do you mean, everything?"

And there it is—the truth about Melor—sitting heavy on my chest. The secret I've been keeping from her, from everyone. If I am pregnant, I'll have to tell her. But right now, I'm not ready to open that can of worms.

"I don't know, it's just... a lot," I say, dodging. Claire seems to sense I'm not ready to spill my guts and hands me some tissues. I wipe my eyes as she tries to lift my mood.

"Look, I was just about to show you the crib," Claire says, pointing across the room. "And check out this super cute diaper bag, I had to have it." She flashes a smile, doing her best to distract me.

I nod, grateful for the effort to take my mind off what could be an absolute life changer. But then I glance at my watch.

Time to face reality.

I pull the test out of my pocket and take a deep breath.

Positive.

The world tilts like it's spinning out of control. My heart races, and everything around me feels too loud, too bright. Claire, sensing I'm on the verge of losing it, quietly guides me over to the rocking chair and gently pushes me down to sit.

"I think I'm having a panic attack," I mutter, my breath coming in short, sharp gasps.

"Hey, deep breaths," Claire says softly, standing in front of me. "In and out. You've got this."

I close my eyes and try to focus on her voice, breathing in deeply, then exhaling slowly. It takes a minute, but the panic starts to subside, and soon enough, I'm back in the moment. When I open my eyes again, I see tears of happiness shining in Claire's.

"Congratulations," she whispers, squeezing my hand.

Oddly, I don't feel bad. In fact, I feel clearheaded, like I can actually think straight for the first time in days. I take another deep breath and say, "I want to make sure. I need to see a doctor."

"Of course," Claire says. "I'll give you the number for my OB. She's great."

She squeezes my hand again and smiles. "Everything's going to be amazing. You're going to be an incredible mom, Am. I just know it."

We hug tightly, and for the first time tonight, I feel a bit of peace. Claire pulls back. "You want me to make up an excuse for you to lie down?"

I shake my head. "No. I'm good."

With that, I stand up, still uncertain, but also, determined.

CHAPTER 23

MELOR

The cold air bites as we step out of Claire and David's place.

I watch Amelia hug Claire tightly, and something about the way Claire whispers, "You've got this," makes me pause. There's a quiet determination in Amelia's eyes, but I know her well enough now to see she's hiding something.

We start walking back to my car, the city around us is quiet and peaceful, wrapped in Christmas lights. Peaceful, at least on the surface. But I can feel the tension radiating off her—like her mind is a million miles away.

"You didn't eat much at dinner," I say, glancing over at her. "You okay?"

She flashes me a smile, one that doesn't reach her eyes. "Yeah, I'm fine. Just wasn't that hungry, I guess."

I don't buy it, but I don't press. I've learned not to push her when she's got something heavy on her mind. She'll come to me when she's ready.

"I like your friends," I say, keeping it light. "And Pancake's got energy for days."

She laughs, a small, quiet sound. "Yeah, Pancake's a trip."

Knowing her thoughts are somewhere else is starting to make me uneasy. I glance up and down the street, always scanning, always aware.

Then, I feel it. A shift in the air. Something's off. I slow down, instinct kicking in, and she mirrors me, confused.

"Keep walking," I say, my voice low. "Act normal."

She hesitates for a second before matching my pace. I feel her heart rate pick up, and her breath quickens. "What's happening?"

I glance back, catching a shadow moving too deliberately. "We're being followed."

Her pulse goes into overdrive, but I keep my voice calm. "Pick up the pace. Now."

I speed up, but she struggles to keep up with my stride. "Melor, your legs—"

"We can't slow down," I say, my tone leaving no room for argument. "We need to get to the car."

I see her eyes widen as it sinks in. She's practically running now, and I glance back again. They're gaining on us.

A slight stream of traffic makes it impossible to cross the street to safety, so I make a quick decision, pulling her into a nearby store that's still open. The neon lights flicker as we walk inside and try to blend in with the late-night browsers.

I move us toward the counter, scanning the store while Amelia pretends to casually look around.

I lean in close, my voice barely a whisper. "Stay calm. We'll be okay."

She nods slightly, but I can feel the fear rolling off her. Inside, I'm ready for whatever's coming. Outside, I stay cool.

I flash a smile at the guy behind the counter, though I can see he's suspicious. Amelia's still out of breath, which doesn't help, but she's quick. All charm, she says, "We just got a new kitten, and of course, we ran out of kitten chow. Little guy eats a lot for something so small."

The guy softens, her words working like magic. "Let me show you where the cat food is."

As they head to the back of the store, I stay at the counter, my eyes on the door and windows. No doubt they're waiting outside, watching. They're not just keeping tabs; they're ready. They're waiting for me to screw up.

They want us to make the first move.

I can feel the tension tightening in my chest. No more time to waste.

I pull out my phone, dialing a number I hoped I wouldn't need to call tonight. It rings once. Twice. Then Mashkov's gruff voice comes through.

"They're here," I say, keeping my voice low and steady. "Two men, watching us right now." I give him my location.

There's a pause. Then, calm as ever, he says, "Stay where you are. I'll handle it."

I hang up, slipping the phone back into my pocket. Mashkov has never let me down before, but I know better than to just wait. I scan the store, calculating every move.

I glance toward the aisle where Amelia is. She's still talking, buying time.

I reach into my coat, fingers curling around the grip of my gun, keeping it hidden but ready. My eyes never leave the front of the store as I move toward the entrance. Amelia's doing exactly what I need her to do—keeping the clerk occupied, charming him with small talk, pulling all of his attention her way.

Through the window, I see two men approaching the store, their steps slow but deliberate. I size them up, noting every detail—the way they're scanning the area, the tension in their posture.

They're hunting.

The last thing I want is a public shootout, but if it comes down to that in order to protect Amelia, there's no question in my mind I'll end it quickly and cleanly. No hesitation.

Fury builds in my chest. I've been watching over her for weeks, but the quiet made me sloppy. Complacent. I know better. I should've anticipated this. I should've said no to dinner.

The men step inside, their eyes immediately sweeping the place. They haven't noticed me yet, but I can feel the tension building. My fingers tighten around my gun. If they make a move, I'm ready.

I shift slightly, positioning myself between them and Amelia. No one touches her. Not while I'm still breathing.

As they step farther in, I brace for the worst, my mind calculating every possible outcome. If it's going to go down, it's going to go down hard, and I'll make sure they regret it. I keep my hand tight on the gun, ready to pull it the second the situation turns.

My eyes remain on both men and within seconds they notice me, but before I can react, they flash their palms, showing they're unarmed. My grip loosens slightly, but I stay on edge, watching their every move.

One of them steps closer, his voice low. "Mashkov sent us."

Relief hits me like a wave, but I don't let it show.

"I'm glad you showed up so fast."

"He had us posted in the neighborhood after your last conversation. Figured a little extra insurance wouldn't hurt."

I can't help but grin. I should've known. Mashkov is always one step ahead.

"We're here to escort you and the lady back to your place," the other man says, his voice all business. "Safer that way."

I glance toward the door, then back at them. "What about the others? Do you know if they're still out there?"

The first man shakes his head. "Saw you had backup and slipped into a car then drove off. But we can't take any chances. They could be regrouping."

They're right. We can't let our guard down. "Let's get out of here," I say as I turn to Amelia, who's still chatting up the clerk, clueless to how close things got.

Time to get her home, where she's safe.

Amelia catches my eye and wraps up her chat with the clerk, her eyes flicking over to the two men with me. Her smile falters, and I can see the worry creeping in. I stride over, keeping everything calm and casual. She doesn't need to know just how close we came to things going sideways.

We head to the counter, and I hand my card to the clerk, giving Amelia a reassuring nod. "Look who I ran into, honey," I say. "They'll be heading over to our place with us."

Her eyes widen slightly but she gets it.

I take the card and bag, giving the clerk a quick smile before turning to Amelia. Together, we walk over to the two men. They fall in step with us as we head out into the cool night.

The air feels heavier now, colder. I'm pissed.

They got too close.

Those bastards were right there, watching, waiting. One wrong move, and it could've been a bloodbath. I clench my jaw, keeping the anger in check.

They won't get another chance.

CHAPTER 24

AMELIA

My heart's racing like I've just sprinted a mile. I glance at the sideview mirror at the two men following our car. Both look like straight-up thugs, with hand and neck tattoos like they just stepped off the set of an action crime movie.

Chatting with the guy at the store about our imaginary kitten helped for a minute, but now with these bodyguards trailing us, the reality of the situation sinks back in.

We're being hunted.

As we turn onto our street, my eyes drift to my little house.

Home.

God, I just want to be back there, snuggled up on my couch, pretending none of this is happening. But I can't.

I can't go home.

The stalkers know where I live. And clearly, they know where I work, too. I clench my jaw, trying to keep it together, but a wave of frustration hits me. My life was normal—baker's hours, coffee shop, chill weekend kind of normal. Now I'm out here dodging assassins with Melor and his backup crew.

And the worst part is I don't know if I'll ever get that normal life back.

We park outside Melor's place and step out of the car. Just as I think I can catch my breath he and the two mob-movie extras begin talking in Russian. It's the first time I've actually heard him speak it, a reminder that he had a whole other life before me, a life that, apparently, isn't done with him yet.

They continue to talk as we step inside the door. One of the guys asks a question to which Melor gratefully replies in English. "My place is a fortress; no one's getting in."

But one of the bodyguards isn't having it. "Mashkov would have our asses if we didn't check thoroughly," he says, deadpan.

Melor concedes—apparently, there's no point in arguing with Mashkov's orders. As the men split off to do their sweep, I stand there, sighing to myself as I head toward the fridge. I spot a bottle of white wine, and for a second, I seriously consider pouring myself a glass. I could really use it after tonight.

But then reality slaps me in the face. Not with a baby growing inside me. No wine, no stress-relieving glass of anything. Just me, my overworked nerves, and this ticking time bomb situation.

I lean against the counter, trying to concentrate on my breathing. I'm not safe. Melor isn't safe. And now, there might be a baby to worry about in the middle of all this.

I shut the fridge door. No wine. Just worries.

Melor comes up beside me, his presence calming, even though my mind's still racing. "I'm sorry you're caught up in this," he says softly. "But I am going to resolve this soon. I promise."

Before I can reply, the men return, speaking in Russian again. It's like nails on a chalkboard, reminding me how much I'm out of the loop of my own life. I roll my eyes and cut in, "Can you please speak English so I can understand? I'm part of this, too. I want to know what's going on."

The men exchange glances, waiting for Melor to give the green light. He nods once. "The house is clear," one of them says. "We're staying in a hotel two blocks away. We'll be in touch if you need us." He hands Melor a business card.

Melor thanks them, and just like that, they're gone, the door clicking shut behind them. The second they're out of sight, I plop into one of the bar seats, tears pricking the corners of my eyes. It's all too much—too much danger, too much uncertainty. I thought I could handle it but now I've got a baby to think about. I don't even know if I can keep myself safe, let alone a tiny human.

I blink, trying to keep the tears from falling, but it's a losing battle. Everything's spiraling, and I don't know how much longer I can fake acting like I've got it under control.

Melor comes over and wraps his arms around me, pulling me close. His warmth and strength are comforting for a second until reality hits again, a new reality. I'm hiding something huge from him. How the hell am I supposed to tell him I'm pregnant?

He holds me tighter, his voice firm. "Everything's going to be fine."

I'm too exhausted to argue. Melor feels the tension in my body and adds, "I promise, Amelia. The problem will be solved by Monday."

I want to believe him, but the sinking feeling in my stomach won't go away. I know he's trying to reassure me, but I also know that promises like that don't always hold up in real life.

"I'm going to do whatever it takes to keep you safe," he murmurs in my ear.

I look up at him, refusing to back down. "No euphemisms, Melor. Be straight with me."

His eyes lock onto mine, fire burning behind those dark pools. "If I have to kill them to protect you, I'll do it. Without hesitation. Without even raising my heart rate."

He says it as if he's discussing something as simple as what to have for dinner. It's chilling, and I believe him. Completely. There's no doubt in my mind that he's telling the truth. The way he says it, so matter-of-factly, makes my stomach flip. I know this is his reality, but it isn't mine.

I swallow hard, "Okay."

Melor wipes away my tears then asks, "Is there anything I can do for you?"

I shake my head because, honestly, I have no clue how to answer that. "No," I mumble.

He kisses me on the cheek, his lips lingering just a second longer than usual. "I'll be in my office making some calls if you need me. Don't hesitate."

Part of me wants to grab his arm and tell him not to leave me alone but I let him go. I need a minute to wrap my head around what happened tonight.

As soon as he's out of sight my mind starts spiraling. I want to keep the baby, but can I really bring a child into Melor's world? The constant danger, the uncertainty; he says he's out of the Bratva, but is that something that anyone can ever truly be free from?

I drag myself out of the chair, thinking maybe I need to eat something, but the thought of food makes my stomach twist even more. I'm still queasy and tonight's events didn't help any.

I head upstairs to the bathroom on the third floor, figuring a bath might calm me down a bit.

I pull off my shirt and catch a glimpse of myself in the mirror. My eyes go straight to my belly.

I know deep in my bones that the test was correct.

Turning on the hot water, I let the tub fill up, the steam curling around me. I strip off the rest of my clothes and slip into the water, sighing as the heat sinks into my skin. I keep telling myself to relax, to breathe, but it's almost impossible. Everything feels so heavy right now.

It's hard not to think about the fact that, before this is all over, someone could end up dead. That's just how things go in Melor's world. He's made that clear.

And now, I'm stuck in the middle of it with a tiny new life to protect.

CHAPTER 25

MELOR

I'm furious with myself.

I can hear the tub running upstairs, the faint sound of water letting me know she's up there, trying to find some peace.

All I can think about is how badly I've fucked this up.

I've dragged her into this mess when all I ever wanted was to leave that life behind. Not only has it returned, but it's pulling her down with it—the first woman I've cared about in a very long time. Hell, if I'm being honest with myself, she could be the *only* woman I've ever felt this way about.

And now I don't know what the fuck to do.

I want to protect her. More than that—I *need* to. I care for her more than I imagined possible after such a short time. She's wrapped herself around my life in a way that goes beyond physical, deeper into a part of me I didn't even know existed. I can no longer imagine my life, or this house, without her in it.

I won't lose her. Not to them. Not like this.

I'll kill anyone who tries.

I'm almost certain that the pair who followed us earlier were the remaining brother and whomever else he's roped into this mess. Both of them have to die. There's no other way. But it's not going to be simple. It will take careful planning and precision, and I'll need help. More than what Mashkov can provide from across an ocean.

A name surfaces in my mind. One from my past. One I swore I'd never say aloud again.

Sasha.

He lives north of the city on a posh estate in Sausalito he bought with his Bratva nest egg. Sasha is perhaps the only man I ever considered a real friend, but our past is dark. We've killed together. We've buried secrets and bodies alike. Reaching out to him means acknowledging that my old life isn't just knocking on the door—it's kicked it down and marched right in.

There's no shortcut out of this.

I take out my phone, scrolling until I find the number I hoped I'd never have to use.

For a second, my thumb hesitates over the screen, but then I press call. The line rings once, twice, before a voice answers, rough and heavily accented in Russian.

"Melor. It's been too long."

My grip tightens on the phone, and I stare at the wall in front of me, knowing that this call is pulling me right back into a world I'd fought so hard to leave behind.

"Indeed, it has," I reply. "I need your help."

∼

I step into Amelia's room. It's past midnight, and she's finally asleep, curled up under the sheets, her breathing steady. I stand there watching her, feeling a mix of emotions that I can't quite place. She looks peaceful, but I know better. The world around her is anything but safe, and I'm the one responsible for that.

After a moment, I turn and leave. There's work to be done.

A half hour later, one of Mashkov's men is posted in front of my house. I head to The Rusted Nail, a dive bar tucked away on 24th Street. The place reeks of cheap beer, stale cigarettes, and desperation. It's dark, the kind of spot where people come to disappear. The flickering neon lights above the bar cast an eerie glow, illuminating the rough edges of this forgotten corner of San Francisco. A few Christmas decorations are hung here and there, almost as an afterthought.

My eyes scan the room until they land on a massive figure sitting at the end of the bar. Though dressed in a sharp jacket, he still looks like he belongs in a cage fight. Tall, burly, and broad-shouldered, the man's sheer size makes him hard to miss.

As if he could feel my presence, Sasha slowly turns toward me, a sly grin spreading across his face. He hasn't changed a bit.

"Melor!" he bellows, his voice booming through the bar. Every head turns, but I keep my eyes locked on him.

Before I can say a word, he's up and wrapping me in a bear hug that crushes the air from my lungs. I laugh, more out of impulse than joy.

"Good to see you, Sasha," I say, pulling back. "You haven't changed a bit."

"Neither have you, brother," he says, and for a moment, it's as if no time has passed.

I size Sasha up again, letting my eyes drift over his sharp, expensive jacket and tailored pants. "Actually, I was wrong. You have changed. What's up with the fancy clothes? They're a far cry from the shit we wore when we were young punks fighting our way out of the gutter."

Sasha throws his head back and laughs, the sound reverberating through the bar. "Let's just say I made a few solid investments over the years. And as far as new looks, I could say the same about you." He smirks, raising an eyebrow. "You're not exactly slumming it these days either."

I grunt, acknowledging the truth. "Fair enough."

We order a couple of whiskeys and find a worn-out booth near the back—dark and dingy, the kind of spot where no one will bother us. Perfect.

We sit down, and Sasha takes a long sip of his drink as he eyes me.

"So, Melor," he says, leaning back, "what the hell's a guy like you been up to? I hear whispers, but it's not like you've been in touch."

I smirk. "You know I left that life behind. I've been busy creating a new life for myself."

Sasha chuckles, shaking his head. "Yeah, I heard. Mr. Straight and Narrow now, huh? Bet it's a hell of a lot different from the old days."

I shrug, taking a sip of my whiskey. "A little quieter, but I make it work. What about you? Living large with that Bratva retirement fund, I see."

He grins. "Yeah, you could say that. Bought myself a nice pad up north. Got the toys, the cash, but it gets boring, you know?"

"Boring, huh?" I raise an eyebrow. "That's a new one for you."

Sasha laughs. "Yeah, well, we're getting old, brother. But you didn't call me just to catch up, did you?"

I glance down at my drink, swirling the liquid before looking back up at him. He's just as sharp as he's always been. "No, I didn't."

Sasha leans in, his expression turning serious. "So, what's going on? You said you needed my help."

I lay it all out for him—Amelia, the home invasion, the assassins. How they've been following us, waiting for the right moment. I admit that I'm stuck. "No matter how many times I replay it in my head, I can't figure out who's behind this," I tell him.

Sasha listens intently, swirling his whiskey with a smirk. When I finish, he lets out an amused chuckle. "I know exactly who it is."

I frown, setting my glass down. "Who?"

He leans back, looking at me like I've missed something obvious. "You don't remember Akim Medvedev?"

I shake my head. "Not really."

"Of course you don't," he says, his voice heavy with amusement. "You weren't the one who had to rough him up before we finished the job; I was."

That jogs my memory. Akim Medvedev was a thief we needed info from. It was starting to come back to me.

Sasha nods, seeing the recognition in my eyes. "That's right. Akim was a piece of work, tough as nails. But what stuck with me was what he said right before you ended him."

I narrow my eyes. "What did he say?"

Sasha's voice drops, taking on that edge of menace I haven't heard in years. "'If you kill me, my brothers will come for you tenfold, no matter how long it takes.'"

I clench my jaw, the weight of the memory settling in. "His brothers."

Sasha nods. "Looks like they finally decided to deliver on that promise."

I sit back, furious with myself for not piecing it together sooner. "How the hell did I miss that?"

"Don't beat yourself up, Melor. We did a lot of dark shit back in the day. Can't expect you to remember every bastard we put down."

"Still," I say, shaking my head. "I should've been able to piece this together." I pause, thinking it through. "You know anything else about the brothers? Where they are now? What they're capable of?"

Sasha nods, taking a sip of his whiskey before answering. "Yeah, I looked into them after we took out Akim. Figured they might come looking for payback someday, so I did my homework."

He leans forward, lowering his voice. "There were two. Denis, the hothead. He's impulsive, reckless, always looking for a fight. He's the type to shoot first, ask questions never."

I nod, remembering bits and pieces now. "And the other?"

"Daniil," Sasha says, his expression darkening. "He's a lot more dangerous, in my opinion. Cool, collected, calculating. He's the brains."

I take that in, feeling the weight of the threat. Denis should be easy—he'll come at me head-on. But Daniil? He's the one I need to worry about, the one who'll wait for the perfect moment to strike.

Sasha's eyes lock onto mine. "If they're coming for you, Melor, it won't be pretty. These brothers don't forget, and they've most likely been planning your demise for years."

"Makes sense. They've been biding their time, waiting for the right moment to strike. They're not going to give up until it's done. I can't afford any missteps or mistakes."

Sasha's eyes narrow. "Who was it you killed in your place? The one who broke in?"

"Some goon. An associate, no doubt. Nothing more."

He grunts, swirling his drink. "That means both brothers are still alive, still coming after you."

I run my hand through my hair, the gravity of it settling over me like a vice. Two relentless brothers with nothing but revenge on their minds. It's not just me they're after now, it's Amelia, too.

Sasha notes my anxiety and his voice softens slightly. "You're in a mess, no doubt. But I've got your back, Melor. You're not in this alone."

I look at him, guilt taking over for a moment. "I'm sorry for dragging you back into this world. I didn't want to—"

He cuts me off. "Don't be. You know I live for this shit. Besides, if they're coming after you, it's only a matter of time before they come for me, too. Might as well get ahead of it."

He leans forward, his eyes hard. "Now let's take the fight to them."

I nod. The game has changed, and I know exactly what I need to do.

CHAPTER 26

AMELIA

I sit in my chambers, torn, my thoughts swirling like a storm I can't control.

The vomiting, the queasiness, it can only mean one thing—I'm pregnant. How did I end up here? Never in a million years did I imagine getting pregnant, especially by a man like him. Yet here I am, carrying the duke's child.

My hand drifts to my stomach, and I can feel the weight of it all settling in. And as if being pregnant wasn't enough, he's away at war, fighting Lord Alistair Blackwood, his greatest rival. Blackwood's been a thorn in his side for years, and now it's erupted into a full-blown war.

What am I to do? I'm stuck here alone in this vast, empty estate, with nothing but my thoughts to keep me company. I feel lost, completely adrift in this new reality.

And to make things worse, I think I might be in love. No, that can't be right. I can't love him. He's a killer, a monster who commands fear and respect in equal measure.

He's the last person I would fall for.

But I can't deny it—the way my heart races when he's near, the way I feel both safe and completely undone in his presence.

I walk to the window, staring out over the moonlit landscape. The world outside may look peaceful, but there's a battle raging inside me.

What do I do? What can I do? He owns my heart and now, my future.

I make a decision—I'm going to tell him, lay it all out. Maybe the duke will prove to be the rogue I suspect he is, the kind of man who wants nothing to do with a bastard child. Or maybe, just maybe, he'll do the right thing.

Images of a royal marriage flash through my mind, unbidden but persistent. I hate that I'm fantasizing about a life with him. But I can't help myself.

I imagine our wedding night, the way he'd look at me when we're finally alone. His hands on my skin, his mouth whispering promises he's never made to anyone else. I picture him over me, in front of a roaring fireplace, his body pressing against mine, his manhood pushing inside, claiming me as his wife in every sense of the word.

Heat floods my cheeks, and I shake my head, trying to snap out of it. This isn't the time for idle fantasies.

I sit down at my desk, pulling out a quill and a sheet of parchment. I'll write to him. Tell him about the child. I'll have the letter sent to the front lines, where he's undoubtedly in the middle of battle.

I stare at the parchment in front of me, quill poised in my trembling hand. My heart pounds as I dip it into the ink, the first words spilling onto the page.

My heart pounds as I begin writing. What will he do when he finds out? Only time will tell. But one thing is certain—there's no turning back now.

Duke,

I write to you with news I never expected to share. I am with child, your child. The very thought of it frightens me, but there is something else I must confess. I love you. I love you more than I can understand or explain. And though my love story did not begin as I had imagined it would, my feelings for you are exactly what I always dreamed love to be.

Tears blur my vision, falling onto the paper as I write. My hand is shaking but I press on, the words coming from the deepest part of me.

You are out there, fighting battles I cannot imagine, and I won't distract you with long letters or ask for anything more than what you can give. But know this: There is a woman back home who loves you, who carries your child, and who prays for your safe return every day.

With trembling fingers, I fold the letter, sealing it with wax. As the seal hardens, I let out a shaky breath. He will soon know the truth.

Letter in hand, I step out of my room. The days of being confined to my quarters ended when things between the duke and me became what they are now. I roam the halls freely, but tonight, my heart is heavy as I make my way down the dimly lit corridor. Candlelight flickers along the stone walls, casting long shadows that seem to stretch endlessly.

I clutch the letter tightly, heading toward the master of the house, Lord Wainright, who will make sure it's sent to the front lines in the morning. From there, I'll have nothing to do but wait. Waiting has never been my strong suit, but I'll have to make do.

As I descend the massive spiral stone staircase, the murmur of voices reaches my ears. They're coming from the main parlor. I hesitate before moving closer, drawn by the low, serious tone. Pressing my ear to the door, I catch snippets of the conversation—the duke is mentioned.

My heart races. Something is wrong.

Without thinking, I push the heavy door open, interrupting the discussion. The fire in the hearth crackles, illuminating the faces of those inside. Lord Wainright stands at the head of the room, along with a trio of soldiers. Leading them is General Castor, one of the duke's most trusted men.

Their faces are grave. The air is thick with tension.

"What's wrong?" I ask, my voice barely above a whisper.

Lord Wainright steps forward, his expression somber. "We've just received word that the duke was slain in battle."

I gasp, the letter slipping from my hand, falling to the floor like a forgotten hope.

I push back from my laptop, and before I know it, tears are streaming down my face. I quickly wipe them away, chalking it up to hormones.

Still, deep down, I know why this entry hit me so hard. I'm pulling from my fears for Melor. He's in danger, just like the duke in my story. And the thought of losing him is too much.

A knock at the door snaps me out of it. "Come in," I say, trying to compose myself.

The door opens and Melor steps into the room. He looks amazing; the moonlight spilling through the window casts him in silver, making him appear supernatural.

He looks at me, concern flickering in his eyes. "What's wrong? You were asleep when I left."

I wave a hand at my laptop, still trying to pull it together. "Oh, nothing. The muse strikes when she strikes."

His expression softens. He knows there's more behind my mood, but he doesn't push.

He walks over and drops onto the couch next to my desk. "I'd love to read it eventually."

I give him a teasing smile. "Maybe I'll hook you up with an advance copy if you're lucky."

He grins, and for a second, it's easy to forget everything else. But then reality seeps back in as it always does. I can't stop myself from asking, "So, where were you?" adding quickly, "I was worried."

He leans over and kisses me, his lips warm and reassuring. "I had to meet a friend," he says. "Everything's fine."

I return the kiss but pull back quickly, narrowing my eyes. "In the middle of the night? Why'd you have to meet him so late?"

For a moment, he looks away like he's unsure how to answer. His jaw tightens, and that familiar wall goes up. I know he's trying to protect me, but damn, it's frustrating when he shuts down like this.

He runs a hand through his hair, glancing away like he's weighing every word he's about to say. "I had to meet with an old friend from my Bratva days. For information."

I blink, my stomach tightening. "What kind of information?"

Instead of answering, he shifts the conversation, his eyes locking on mine. "Do you want a life together?"

I freeze. Did I hear him right?

"Do I... want a life together?" I repeat dumbly, as if saying the words aloud will help me process them. "With you?"

"Yes. That's what I'm asking."

I sit there stunned, trying to catch up.

"If that's what you want, Amelia, then it can happen. But there are things from my past, things I need to take care of. I hate that they've resurfaced but they have, and they need to be dealt with. I want to keep you as far away from all of it as possible."

His words hang in the air between us, heavy with meaning. I don't know what to say, and for a second, I feel completely out of my depth. A life together? With him? And everything that comes with it?

He holds out his hand, a silent offer. Without thinking, I take it, letting him pull me over to the couch. The moment

I'm close to him, his warmth and his presence instantly make me feel better.

I'm absolutely stunned by this new revelation. My brain is doing backflips, and I have no idea what to say. So, I blurt out the only thing that comes to mind. "Do *you* want a life with *me*?"

He grins that sexy little grin that drives me crazy, and without a word, he leans in, pressing his lips to mine. His kiss is his answer, and it's all the answer I need.

He pulls back, that damn grin still on his face. "I hope that answered your question."

I smirk, my heart racing. "Oh, it sure did. But I've got some follow-ups."

I'm on him in an instant, our lips crashing together. His hands grip my waist as mine slide up into his hair, tugging just enough to make him groan against my mouth.

This is the kind of moment where everything else fades. Just me and him, no past, no Bratva, no danger—just *us*.

We start on the couch, lips locked, hands roaming, but it's not enough. Without a word, we shift toward the window, where the moonlight spills in, casting a soft, silvery glow over everything. It's the kind of lighting that makes it feel unreal, too perfect to be happening.

He's behind me before I can catch my breath, his body heat melting into mine. I feel his hands on my hips, strong, commanding. Before I know it, he's slipping into me, his cock filling me up, that delicious stretch I can never get enough of. I let out a shaky moan, pushing back against him, needing more.

He tugs my hair, hard enough to make me gasp, but just enough to keep it on that perfect edge between pleasure and pain.

"You like that, don't you?" he murmurs against my ear, his voice low and rough, sending a wave of heat through me. "You love how I make you feel."

A shiver runs down my spine as I brace myself against the window frame, staring out at the city glowing in the moonlight. But all I can focus on is him, his body pressed tight against mine, the way he fills me so completely.

He drives into me harder, his grip tightening on my hips. "Look at you," he growls, his voice thick with need. "Your pussy's so perfect. So fucking perfect for me."

My breath catches in my throat as the pleasure builds. "Melor..." I manage to whisper, half lost in the feeling, my body trembling as he moves against me, each thrust more intense than the last.

"You love how I fuck you, don't you?" he asks, his one hand pulling my hair just enough to make me arch. "Tell me how much you love it."

"So much," I gasp, completely lost to him. "I love the way you fuck me, the way you fill me up." His cock drives into me, pushing me closer and closer to the edge.

"Then beg for it," his voice a rough command against my skin.

And I do, my voice breathless. "Please, Melor... please."

He keeps going, his rhythm relentless, his dirty talk only fueling the fire. "You're so close, aren't you?" he growls, his voice thick with need. "I can feel it. Come for me, baby. I want to feel you come all over my cock."

I crash into the orgasm, my body tightening around him as waves of pleasure wash over me. My moans fill the room, and I can't help but beg him to come with me, but he's not done yet.

I turn around and we kiss again, deep and hungry, before I pull back just enough to meet his eyes. "Take off your clothes and go sit on the couch," I whisper.

I smile at him mischievously as his own grin widens, as he slips out of his clothes, moving to the couch like I told him to.

I watch him, my eyes lingering on his gorgeous, hard cock, standing tall and ready for me.

"Ask nicely," I tease, my smile turning playful.

He chuckles. "Pretty please? With sugar on top."

With that, I lower myself down, his cock sliding inside me, splitting me in two in the best possible way.

CHAPTER 27

MELOR

"Fuck, Amelia."

She's on top of me, starting to ride, and all I can do is watch her.

The way she moves, the way she looks at me—God, it's too much. I've never been the kind of man to let someone else take control, but with her, I want it. I *need* it.

My hands grip her hips as she starts to move. Her heat surrounds me, and every time she slides down, it's like she's pulling me deeper into something I can't escape—something I don't *want* to escape.

"You feel so fucking good," I mutter, my voice rough, almost desperate. I'm not used to feeling this way, this vulnerable. I'm a man who dominates, who takes what he wants, but with Amelia, it's different. She's different.

She's so wet, and every time she slides down onto me, I'm drowning in the heat of her. The sight of my cock disappearing into her perfectly tight pussy over and over is enough to drive me insane. Her hips roll, and her body arches. She's in complete control, and I can't take my eyes off her.

I run my hands over her thighs, her ass, pulling her tighter against me. I'm caught up in her. Trapped. Every movement she makes is like a drug, and I can't get enough.

"God, you're fucking beautiful," I mutter. I mean it, too—not just how she looks but how she moves, the control she takes, the power she wields.

It turns me on even more watching her take what she wants, her confidence making me lose my own control. She's got me right where she wants me, and I love every damn second of it.

Her body's a masterpiece, and I'm losing myself in her.

I can feel myself getting closer, the tension coiling in my core, but I don't want it to end yet.

Just then she leans forward, her hands on my chest, her pace relentless, and it hits me all at once. I'm not just fucking her—I'm falling for her. It's overwhelming, the physical pleasure mixing with deep emotions. It scares the hell out of me.

"Melor..." she breathes, her voice soft and breathless, and it sends a shockwave through me. She arches her back, her body tightening around me, and I can feel her teetering on the edge. My hands cup her perfect breasts, fingers brushing her hardened nipples, and I can't take it anymore.

Together, we crash over the edge. Her body clenches around me and I feel her shudder, her moans getting louder as she rides out her release. It's enough to send me spiraling, my own orgasm hitting me like a freight train. The world fades, and it's just the two of us, completely wrapped in each other, lost in the moment.

Her back arches further, pressing her chest into my hands, and I grip her tighter, holding her close as I fill her, my body shaking with the intensity of it.

As the waves of pleasure slowly begin to settle, my heart is pounding, not just from the high, but from the realization that I'm not just lost in the sex. I'm lost in *her*. I didn't expect this—didn't expect her to mean this much. But she does.

After we come down from the high, she stays on top of me, her body still pressed against mine, my cock still inside her. I hold her close, my arms wrapped around her like I never want to let go. And part of me doesn't. The thought of holding her like this forever—it's tempting in ways I never expected to feel.

I kiss her, deep and slow, tasting the satisfaction on her lips. Eventually, she pulls back, climbing off me, and the moment our bodies separate, I already miss the warmth of her. She moves around the room, closing her laptop, drawing the curtains halfway.

The fatigue of the day suddenly hits me like a heavy weight, and I lean back on the couch, letting my eyes close for just a second, listening to the soft sounds of her moving.

"We should probably get to bed," she says softly, her voice tugging me from the edge of sleep.

I chuckle, eyes still closed. "I could easily fall asleep right here." I gesture for her to join me, and she doesn't hesitate.

She climbs onto the couch, the soft cushions big and cozy enough to hold us both. She rests her head on my chest, her body fitting against mine like she was made for me. I kiss her again, slower this time, letting myself savor every second.

As I lay there, her head rising and falling with each of my breaths, I'm overwhelmed with the feelings coursing through me. This is more than I thought I could ever have or deserved.

And it terrifies me.

I'm holding her close, her body nestled against mine, both of us teetering on the edge of sleep. The room is quiet, save for the soft rhythm of her breathing and the occasional sounds of the city outside.

Then, she mumbles something, barely audible.

I lean closer, brushing her hair aside. "What did you say?"

Her eyes are closed but she mumbles it again, a little clearer this time. My heart stops when I hear it—*I love you*. She's half-asleep so she might not even be aware of what she said.

The weight of her words settles over me. I don't deserve her love. She's tangled up in my world now, a world I never wanted her to be a part of. Will she feel the same when she's fully awake and not drifting off in my arms?

The truth is, I love her, too. More than I ever thought possible. But I won't say it now. Not when she won't remember it. When I tell her, she's going to hear it, feel it. It will be real, not some whispered words in the dark.

I kiss her forehead, breathing her in, my hand resting against the curve of her back. Her body softens in my arms, completely relaxed, trusting.

I hold her tighter, letting my eyes close, and for the first time in a long time, I fall asleep without feeling like the weight of the world is on my shoulders.

CHAPTER 28

AMELIA

I wake up early, a weird, nervous energy buzzing through me.

I look around and realize we're in his bed—he must've carried me here at some point during the night.

I glance over at him, still sleeping soundly, his face relaxed in a way I rarely see, and I can't help but smile. But then my hand instinctively goes to my belly, bracing for the nausea that's been my lovely morning companion lately.

But there's nothing.

At first, I'm relieved, but then that relief turns into a nagging worry. Does no nausea mean no baby? My mind races, and I know I need to see a doctor—soon. I can't just sit in limbo, wondering what's going on inside me.

I quietly slip out of bed, making my way downstairs to the kitchen. It's still early, the sun barely peeking over the horizon, casting soft light through the windows. Everything feels so calm. I throw together something simple for breakfast—oatmeal and fruit.

I sit at the counter, stirring my oatmeal, grateful for the day off but also feeling like there's a ticking clock in the back of my mind. I need answers. And I need them fast.

When I hear his footsteps coming down the stairs, my heart does a little jump of joy. God, I can't ever remember feeling this way about a guy before. It's like I'm hyper-aware of him, and it's terrifying and wonderful all at once.

"Morning," he says, giving me a quick peck on the cheek as he passes. It's simple, but meaningful.

He starts boiling water for the French press, then glances at me. "I don't want to pry," he says casually but with that undertone of concern I'm getting used to. "But are you okay?"

I feign confusion, playing it off. "What do you mean?"

"At Claire and David's. You seemed off, like you were sick."

"Oh, right." I wave away his concern, trying to appear nonchalant. "I'm fine. Must've been something I ate."

He doesn't seem convinced, but he doesn't push. Typical Melor—always sensing when something's up but letting me come to him when I'm ready.

I take a few bites of my oatmeal, chewing slowly and praying I keep it down. No nausea, so maybe I'm good. But it's not the nausea that's making me nervous right now. It's what I said last night. I told him I loved him. I remember mumbling it, and I remember him not saying it back.

I need to talk to him about that. But... when? And how do I bring it up?

I decide there's no point in dragging this out. I take a deep breath, steeling myself. "Did you hear me last night?"

Melor glances up from his coffee, lowering the iPad he reads the morning news on. He nods but doesn't say anything. Not a word.

"I meant it," I say, my voice a little firmer than I intended. "I love you."

He looks down at his coffee, and my heart skips a beat. No. *No.*

My stomach twists as reality hits. He doesn't love me. This is just a fling to him and here I am, falling in love Ike an idiot.

I bite the inside of my cheek, forcing myself to stay composed when all I want to do is cry. My voice comes out tight, but I manage to say it. "If you don't feel the same, it's fine. I just needed you to know."

He says, "Okay," then thanks me for telling him.

He's thanking me?

I blink at him, my chest tightening. I open my mouth but stop myself. What can I say?

I try to brush it off, but the words stick in my throat. He thanked me like I just handed him a cup of coffee, not my freaking heart.

My appetite is gone. I get up and carry my half-finished oatmeal over to the sink. Tears prick the corners of my eyes, but I fight them back. I feel like a complete idiot.

Before I can sink any deeper into the hole I'm digging for myself, his arms wrap around my middle from behind, pulling me close.

I close my eyes as his body presses against me. Damn him. I hate that I'm pissed, but all I want in this moment is to melt into him, to feel the safety of his arms around me.

How does this man have so much power over me? It's like he's got a direct line to my heart and can push every button without even trying.

His hands move to my hips, turning me around gently, and I find myself looking up into those stormy gray eyes of his. I feel safe and terrified all at once, like I'm about to step off a cliff without knowing if he'll catch me.

He leans down and kisses me softly. Tears slip down my cheeks before I can stop them, and when he pulls back, he slowly and gently wipes them away with his thumbs.

I start to feel a little better but I'm still in this weird limbo, wondering what the hell is going on in his head and how he feels about me.

Then, finally, he speaks, his voice low and confident. "I love you, too."

The words hit me like a tidal wave, washing away all my doubts and worries. He said it. My heart stumbles, and for a moment, I forget to breathe.

He looks down at me and says, "I love you" again like he's making sure I heard him. "I didn't expect it. I didn't plan for it. But it's happened. What started out as wanting to protect you has turned into so much more."

I can feel my heart swelling with happiness. He continues, "It's terrifying, to be honest. Thrilling, too. You make me feel things I didn't think I'd ever feel again."

I smile, happy tears slipping from my eyes. Before I know it, I'm full-on sobbing, my face buried in his shoulder. He holds me close, his strong arms wrapped around me, anchoring me in place.

"I'm sorry," I manage between sobs, my voice cracking. "I'm such a mess."

He kisses the top of my head and rubs my back gently. "You're allowed to be a mess now and again, Amelia. My job is to be here for you, to protect you, and I'll do that every way I can."

His words are soothing, wiping away my doubts. I pull back just enough to look at him, and I feel a mix of relief and love wash over me. This is real; what we have is real, and for the first time in a long time, I feel safe knowing he's by my side.

I stand on my tiptoes and kiss him, and he kisses me right back, deep and slow, making my head spin. He scoops me up, lifting me off the floor, and carries me toward the bedroom.

He lays me down gently on the bed, his lips trailing over my skin, making me shiver. Slowly, he peels off my sleeping shorts and panties, his touch sending little sparks of electricity through me. I sit up, tugging my shirt over my head, and catch a glimpse of my boobs. They seem bigger.

As I'm lost in that thought, I notice him looking at me, his brow slightly furrowed.

"What's up?" I ask, raising an eyebrow.

"You look different somehow," he says, his voice laced with curiosity, "even more beautiful."

I melt, feeling my heart do a little flip at his words, though, deep down, I can't shake the feeling that he's starting to suspect something. But then his lips are on me again, and all my thoughts scatter. Right now, I'm focused on this moment. The rest can come later.

He takes off his shirt and tosses it aside, then lies down next to me, his body warm against mine. His hand slips between my legs, fingers brushing over me in that way that drives me crazy. His touch is gentle at first, teasing, making me ache for more.

"You're so fucking perfect," he whispers, his voice husky and filled with need.

I bite my lip, already losing myself in him. He slides his fingers over my clit, moving in slow, tantalizing circles, building the tension. My breath catches as his touch gets firmer, more insistent, but still careful, like he's savoring every second of this.

He kisses me, soft and slow, his lips lingering on mine as I moan against his mouth. Every little movement of his fingers pushes me closer, my body trembling beneath his touch.

"Come for me," he murmurs, his lips brushing my ear.

I'm right there, teetering on the edge, and with one last slow, deliberate stroke, he pushes me over. My back arches, and I let out a shaky moan as I come to his touch, the orgasm rippling through me. His fingers keep working me, drawing out every last bit of pleasure until I'm gasping for breath.

The wave fades, leaving me warm and flushed, but I want more, I *need* more. I pull him closer, my body already craving him again.

CHAPTER 29

MELOR

"You're getting good at this," I say as I watch her pull down my zipper. "I love how much you're taking control."

There's something different about her tonight. It's subtle but it's there. I can't put my finger on it, though. It's like that old cliché about how loving someone makes them more beautiful, and fuck, do I love her.

Before I can overthink it, her hand reaches down, wrapping around my cock. Instantly, I'm yanked out of my head and back into the moment. She strokes me slowly, her touch firm and confident, and I can't tear my eyes away.

She smirks up at me, playful as always. "Guess I've learned from someone who's pretty bossy between the sheets."

I grunt in response, but I can't help the grin tugging at my lips. "Guess I'll have to teach you a few more things, then."

She leans down, her tongue teasing the tip of my manhood before trailing all the way down to the root. I groan, my hand instinctively tangling in her hair as she takes her time, savoring every inch of me.

My heart pounds as all thoughts disappear. All I can focus on is her—how good she feels, how much I need her, and how she's managing to take control of me all over again.

"God, you're sexy," I murmur as I watch her, mesmerized by how focused she is, how much she seems to enjoy this. It drives me wild, knowing she's doing this because she wants to, not because she feels she has to.

She looks up at me, her eyes locking with mine for just a second, and the sight of her lips around me nearly pushes me over the edge. I groan again, my hips bucking slightly as she takes me deeper.

"You feel so good, baby," I whisper, my hand tightening in her hair, guiding her just a little. "I love how you make me feel."

I'm falling harder for her with every touch, every breath, every moment I spend with her. And not just during sex.

She picks up the pace, her mouth moving faster, and I can feel it—I'm right there, ready to lose it. My breath hitches, my body tightens, but I don't want it to end yet. Not like this. With a groan, I reach down, gently guiding her off my cock. She looks up at me, lips swollen, a mix of lust and curiosity in her eyes.

"Almost made me finish. You're too fucking good at that."

A wicked smile crosses her face. "I love the way you taste," she says, her voice sultry and teasing. "And I love watching you when I'm working you like that."

"Yeah?" I murmur, brushing my thumb across her bottom lip. "Well, I love how you look when I'm buried inside you."

Her smile softens, and it hits me again—how much I love her. I lean down and kiss her, pouring everything I'm feeling into it. She melts into me, and I guide her onto the bed, pulling her close in a spoon position.

I slide into her from behind, her body fitting perfectly against mine, and a groan escapes my lips. I wrap my arms around her, my hands roaming her body as I kiss her neck, her shoulder, savoring every second of this.

She feels incredible, but more than that—she feels like home.

Her breath comes in soft moans, her body reacting to every move I make. She's laid bare before me—her back arched, the curve of her hips pressed against me, every inch of her trembling with need.

"You feel so damn good," I whisper against her neck, my lips grazing her skin. "So beautiful, so perfect."

Her body starts to shake, her moans turning into breathless cries, and I can feel her clenching around me, on the edge of losing control. I hold her tighter, kissing her neck, murmuring loving words as I drive her right to the brink. Her body quivers, and then she breaks, coming hard around my cock.

I climb over her, pulling out just long enough to position myself on top. I take in the sight of her beneath me—her lips parted, her chest rising and falling, her hair splayed out over the pillow. She's the most beautiful thing I've ever seen.

"You're so goddamn gorgeous," I murmur, leaning down to kiss her again.

She blushes at my words, and it only makes her sexier. She gives me a playful smirk, her eyes gleaming. "You're not so bad yourself."

Her hands slide to my ass, gripping me with a teasing squeeze. "How long are you going to make me wait?" she whispers, her voice laced with desire.

With a groan, I push inside her, burying myself deep.

I start thrusting harder, the sound of her soft moans driving me wild. Every breath, every sigh she makes only pulls me further into her, my body responding to hers in ways I can barely control. Her hands grip my shoulders, her nails digging in as her body starts to tremble beneath me. I know she's close—so close—and I want to take her right over the edge yet again.

"Come for me."

Her moans get louder, her body tensing as I keep driving into her, harder, faster. She lets go, her orgasm crashing over her, her body tightening around me. I can feel every pulse, every shudder as she grips me, her pleasure flooding through her, and it's enough to take me with her.

I explode inside her, my body tightening, every nerve lighting up. The feeling of her squeezing me, the warmth, the intensity, it's all overwhelming. I empty into her, the pleasure so intense there's nothing else, just the two of us.

I stay inside her, my lips trailing soft kisses over her face, her neck, her shoulders. I don't want to let go of this moment.

When I finally slide out, I pull her close, wrapping her up in my arms.

"I love you," I whisper, "more than anything."

As she comes down from her high, I catch a very subtle shift in her mood.

"What's going on?" I ask.

She bites her lip, then shakes her head. "Never mind; it's nothing."

"Are you sure?"

She glances away, her fingers playing with the edge of the sheet. "I'm just worried."

I tighten my grip around her, pulling her closer. "You're safe here."

She shakes her head softly. "I'm not worried about me. I'm worried about *you*."

That catches me off guard. I brush my lips against her neck, letting out a breath. "I'll be fine," I assure her. "I'm working with Sasha. We've got solid leads, and we're getting to the bottom of it. I'm not letting them get close again."

She seems to relax a little at that, but I can still sense there's more on her mind. Something deeper she's not ready to share. I don't push.

Instead, I keep holding her, my hand stroking her side, tracing soft patterns along her skin. Slowly, her breathing evens out, and she drifts off to sleep, warm and safe in my arms.

I gently ease out of bed, careful not to wake her, pulling on some clothes before heading downstairs.

The house is quiet, and I find myself standing in the kitchen, staring at the calendar on the wall. Christmas is just around the corner. A part of me wonders what it would feel like to spend it with her, all of this danger behind us.

What a perfect Christmas gift it would be to have this nightmare over, to know she's truly safe.

I pour myself a cup of coffee, the warmth spreading through my chest as I take a sip. But my mind keeps drifting back to Sasha. I need to hear from him soon, to get the next steps locked down. We can't afford to lose momentum.

A chime from my phone interrupts my thoughts, the familiar alert from the Ring cam app. I pull it up, bringing up the view of the front door. Nothing. The porch is empty.

Frowning, I grab my gun from the counter, heading toward the front door. I open it slowly, scanning the area. No one's there.

Then, out of nowhere, a little black kitten appears, padding up to the porch as if he owns the place.

I laugh under my breath, shaking my head. So, this is what set off the alert? The kitten doesn't even hesitate, he walks right inside like he belongs here.

I'm about to shoo the little guy back out when something stops me. The cat food we picked up at the store earlier flashes through my mind. With a shrug, I head into the kitchen, the kitten following close behind, its tiny paws padding along behind me.

I grab the bag from the counter, shaking it slightly as I open it. The kitten's ears perk up, and it lets out a tiny meow, eager for the meal. I grab a bowl, pour some of the food in, add a bowl of water, and set both down on the floor.

The kitten pounces on it like it hasn't eaten in days, digging in with its little face buried in the bowl. I lean back against the counter, arms crossed, watching the scene unfold.

Thinking about Amelia's "lie" earlier that we needed cat food settles in. It's as if she knew the universe was sending us a kitten.

CHAPTER 30

AMELIA

I wake up late the next morning, my stomach doing somersaults.

Great. The nausea's back. I barely make it to the bathroom before I throw up. My head spins as I flush the toilet, wiping my mouth with the back of my hand.

I need to go to the doctor and confirm what the test said, though, at this point, I know in my gut its true.

I splash some water on my face and go to find Melor.

He's in his office, pacing with his phone pressed to his ear. I stop at the doorway, catching snippets of the conversation.

"...need to know where they are... no, we can't wait until it's too late. You understand?"

His tone is dark, serious, and dangerous. Whoever's on the other end, it's clear the conversation is heavy. But then his eyes land on me, and he immediately knows something's up. He ends the call, not even bothering to say goodbye.

"What's wrong?" he asks, his eyes locked on mine, concern written all over his face.

I take a deep breath. "I need to see a doctor."

Before Melor can respond, I catch a glimpse of something that makes me do a double take. Curled up on the leather couch is a tiny black kitten.

I walk over slowly, half-expecting it to vanish like some strange hallucination. But nope, there really is a tiny black kitten there, curled up and fast asleep, purring softly.

I sit down carefully next to the little thing, reaching out to pet him—or her—gently. "Where did *you* come from?"

"Sort of invited himself in," Melor says from behind me. I glance up at him, raising an eyebrow. "I went to check on something outside, and there he was. We had the cat food from last night, so I figured I'd feed him."

I laugh softly, still stroking the kitten's silky fur. "You just let a stray cat waltz in and get comfortable?"

Melor shrugs, leaning against his desk, arms crossed. "He made himself at home. What was I supposed to do?"

The kitten purrs louder under my hand and I smile, the tiny ball of fur distracting me from my nausea. "So does this mean he's going to stay?"

Melor's gaze softens as he looks at the kitten. "Seems like he's already decided that."

I giggle, the moment bringing a little lightness to the anxiety swirling in my chest.

The kitten looks up at me, his little face scrunched up in that adorably sleepy way, and I melt.

"If the cat's going to stay," Melor says, his tone teasing but with a serious edge, "he's going to need two things."

"What's that?" I ask, still petting the tiny furball.

"A litter box, first and foremost, and a name."

I look down at the kitten, taking in his dark fur and thinking of the way he just wandered in and made himself at home. "Duke," I say, thinking of the character from my book. "He looks like a Duke to me."

Melor chuckles, nodding. "Duke it is."

But then his expression shifts back to concern. "Now, about that doctor," he presses, his eyes locking onto mine.

I freeze for a moment, hating the lie I'm about to tell, but I don't want to jump the gun and say anything before I know for sure. "My stomach has really been bothering me," I say, forcing a casual shrug. "It's probably nothing, but I'd rather be safe than sorry."

He narrows his eyes slightly, like he's reading between the lines, but he doesn't push.

"It's Saturday," I add, trying to sound nonchalant. "We can wait until Monday to—"

But Melor's already shaking his head, pulling out his phone. "I know a place that does Saturday appointments," he says. He starts dialing without even giving me a chance to argue.

An hour later, we're pulling up to a quiet little doctor's office tucked away in Noe Valley. The building is small and unassuming, with ivy crawling up the brick walls and a wooden sign that looks like it's been there for ages. Not the kind of place you'd expect to have a last-minute appointment on a Saturday, but Melor knows people, so here we are.

Before I can even reach for the door handle, Melor is already out of the car, scanning the street. I watch him, knowing he's armed and that his eyes are peeled for any sign of danger.

We go inside and sit in the waiting room, the soft hum of a saltwater fish tank fills the quiet space. I glance around and notice the receptionist and another female patient sneaking glances at Melor. It makes me chuckle and also feel good.

I lean over, whispering, "Looks like you've got some admirers."

He smirks. "You're the only one I care about admiring me."

A nurse steps out and calls my name.

"I'll be here," he says as I follow her to an exam room.

A few minutes after the nurse takes my vitals and asks me the basic questions, the door opens. The doctor steps in, exuding calm confidence. She's middle-aged and sharp, with that no-nonsense vibe that tells me she's seen it all and isn't rattled by much.

"Hi, I'm Dr. Melanie Harris," she says, giving me a reassuring smile as she sits down across from me.

"Amelia," I reply, my voice a little shaky. "Nice to meet you."

"Nice to meet you, too, Amelia," she says warmly, glancing at her tablet. "Let's see what's going on, shall we?"

Her tone is calm and professional, and it instantly puts me at ease. This might not be so bad after all.

I take a deep breath, feeling the words tumble out of my mouth before I can even think about them. "I think I'm pregnant," I blurt out. "I've been feeling nauseous, throwing up, and I've been absolutely terrible about taking my birth control. I took a home test and it came out positive."

She holds up a hand, calming me down instantly with that steady, professional energy. "Alright, let's take it one step at a time. First, we'll do a pregnancy test here to confirm. I'll also order bloodwork."

She stands, handing me a cup. "Once we know the results, we'll be better able to diagnose what's causing your symptoms."

I head to the bathroom, do my business, and hand the sample to a nurse, my heart racing the whole time. Back in the room, I nervously wait, my leg bouncing uncontrollably. Dr. Harris comes back in with a smile on her face, and my stomach drops.

"Well, Amelia," she says, "it's confirmed, you're pregnant."

The room starts spinning and I can't catch my breath. My chest tightens, and I'm afraid I might be having a panic attack.

Dr. Harris notices immediately. "Breathe, Amelia. It's okay. Just take some deep breaths. In and out slowly; that's it."

I do as she says, inhaling deeply and exhaling slowly until the spinning stops and I feel my pulse slow down.

Dr. Harris gives me a gentle look. "You'll want to make an appointment with your OB/GYN soon."

I nod, still trying to wrap my head around everything.

"Is the father in the picture?" she asks gently.

"Yes."

Dr. Harris gives me a warm smile as she stands up, grabbing a pamphlet from the counter.

She hands me the pamphlet along with a little card full of phone numbers. "Here are some resources, places you can call if you need help, have questions, or just need someone to talk to. There's no rush to figure it all out, but it's important to have support, especially if you're feeling overwhelmed."

I glance at the numbers. Counseling, prenatal care, a support group. "Thanks," I say, offering a weak smile.

She smiles back at me. "You've got this, trust me. Just make sure you take care of yourself, and that will take care of the baby."

I step back into the waiting room to find Melor on the phone again. I quickly shove the pamphlet and card Dr. Harris gave me deep into my bag, not wanting him to see it. He spots me, and just like that, he ends the call and walks over, eyes full of concern.

He wraps an arm around me as we leave the office.

"How are you feeling?"

I force a smile, trying to keep my cool. "Doctor said it's probably just a bug. Gotta let it run its course."

He nods, but his expression doesn't soften. "I'll make you some mushroom and potato soup when we get home. It's an old favorite from my childhood. It always made me feel better."

My heart warms at that, and I can't help but smile as we walk to the car, his hand wrapped around mine. It feels nice, normal even, but inside, I'm a complete mess. How long can I keep this secret from him?

I glance at him as we get in the car, his gaze looking cautiously up and down the street. I can't tell him about the baby. Not yet. Not when he's already dealing with so much. He needs to be able to concentrate so he doesn't make a fatal mistake.

CHAPTER 31

MELOR

It's late and Amelia has already gone to bed. The house is quiet.

I sit in my office, the glow of my laptop lighting up the darkened room. On the screen is Mashkov, his hard features etched with years of violence and wisdom. His silver hair is cropped close, his face set in lines that speak of a life lived in the shadows. He's in his sixties, but he's still sharp, still dangerous.

"I've sent you everything I've got," Mashkov says. "Daniil Medvedev's in Oakland. Looks like he's been laying low there for a while."

I nod, scanning the info. Oakland is close, close enough that it's no wonder the Medvedev brothers thought they could take me out. They've been right under my nose.

"We think living near you gave them the idea to finally make their move," Mashkov continues, his gaze sharp as ever. "But all I've got is the address. No other intel."

"That's enough," I reply. "I'm going to kill him."

Mashkov raises an eyebrow. "And how exactly do you plan to do that? Have you secured backup?"

"Bogdnan's coming with me," I say, my tone leaving no room for doubt. "We'll handle it."

Mashkov leans back, a ghost of a smirk crossing his face. "Good. Daniil seems slippery, but if anyone can handle this, it's you two. Anyway, good luck, Melor. You'll need it."

I shake my head, eyes cold. "I don't need luck. I need Daniil dead."

Mashkov chuckles darkly. "As always, you're straight to the point. Just keep your head clear."

"I will."

I stand, my mind already shifting to what comes next. I cross the room to the large landscape painting on the wall. I slide the canvas aside, revealing the hidden safe behind it.

Opening it, I grab what I need. First, my Glock 19, reliable and discreet. Then, the H&K MP5, compact but deadly when things get close and ugly. I pull out a tactical knife as well, securing it in my belt. Lastly, I strap on a bulletproof vest. I'm going into this fully prepared. Daniil Medvedev is going to die tonight.

My phone buzzes with a text from Sasha.

Outside.

I reply.

On my way.

Before leaving, I step into the bedroom where Amelia's sleeping soundly, her soft breaths barely audible. Something feels off. She's been distant, and I know she's hiding something from me. That much was clear by the look on her face as we left the doctor's office.

I watch her for another moment, debating whether to wake her up, press her for the truth. But there's no time for that now. Whatever it is, we'll deal with it once this mess is over.

I head downstairs and see Duke curled up in a tight ball on one of the couches. On the other couch, the two men Mashkov sent the other night are keeping watch. One of them nods at Duke. "You got a new recruit?"

I chuckle softly. "Keep an eye on him—and Amelia."

They nod, and without another word, I step outside, locking the door behind me. The night is cold.

The real work begins now.

I spot Sasha's car across the street and head over, slipping into the passenger seat without a word. He pulls away smoothly, the engine barely making a sound in the quiet night.

"You dig up anything on Daniil?" I ask, eyes scanning the empty streets as we leave San Francisco behind.

Sasha shakes his head. "Not much. He's been a ghost for the last several years. No movement, no chatter. It's like he's vanished off the radar."

The city blurs past us, the chilly winter air pressing against the windows. Christmas lights twinkle along the streets as we drive, casting colorful reflections in the darkened glass.

San Francisco is calm at night, almost peaceful. But that changes the moment we cross into Oakland. The streets are darker and more dangerous.

We pull into Daniil's neighborhood. A small and modest single-family home sits at the corner with a "For Sale" sign out front. No Christmas decorations, just a few lights on inside, hinting at a normal life within. It looks like the kind of place someone would hide, thinking they'd blend in.

Sasha glances over at me as we park. "In and out. Drop him and we're gone. Shouldn't take longer than five minutes if we do it right."

I nod, my hand resting on the Glock at my side. "Five minutes."

We sit in the car, watching the house in silence, doing a quick recon. The neighborhood is quiet, and we have a clear view through the front windows. Then, we see him. Tall, slim, slicked-back hair, moving with the kind of casual confidence that says he doesn't think anyone's looking for him.

That mindset only benefits us.

"That's our guy," Sasha mutters beside me, his voice low. "That's him."

I tense, ready to move, my hand gripping the Glock in my lap. But then, something catches my eye. A woman steps into view, mid-thirties, pretty. I raise my binoculars, focusing on her. She's wearing a ring on her finger.

"Married," I say, spotting a matching ring on Daniil's hand.

And then, another surprise. Two kids, toddlers, twins by the look of them, run into the room, laughing as they chase each other around. My gut twists.

"Man's got a family," Sasha says quietly, shaking his head. "I didn't know."

I lower the binoculars, jaw clenched. "We can't kill him right now."

Sasha looks at me, surprised. "What?"

"We don't kill a man in front of his family." I sigh, running my hand through my hair.

"What about the other brother? Denis?"

"He was the one at my house that night. I don't know where he lives."

He exhales, leaning back in his seat. "So, what's the plan?"

I glance back at the house. "Simple. We go up and have a little chat."

Sasha laughs, a deep, rumbling sound. "A chat, huh?"

"Hide your weapons," I say, smirking. "And try to look friendly."

Sasha flashes a big, over-the-top smile. "Friendly enough for you?"

I chuckle. "Not *that* friendly; that's creepy."

We tuck away our guns and approach the front door, Sasha and I keeping our movements casual. I knock twice, and a few moments later, Daniil answers. His eyes flicker with recognition the second he sees us. He stiffens, his face draining of color.

"What is this?" he asks, his voice tight with fear. His eyes dart between us, already knowing what's coming.

We say nothing.

His expression falls completely. "I'm not in that life anymore. I have a family. Please."

I raise my hands, palms up, trying to keep the situation calm. "We're not here for anything like that. We just want to chat."

Daniil's wife steps into view, concern etched across her face. "What's going on?" she asks, glancing at us cautiously, like we're about to pull guns at any second.

"A chat," I say, hearing the faint sound of the kids laughing and playing in the background.

Daniil turns to his wife. "Everything's fine. Just keep an eye on the kids."

She hesitates, her hand lingering on the door. "Should I call—?"

"No," he cuts her off sharply. "It's just a chat."

After a tense pause, she nods and walks back inside, but not without casting one last wary glance in our direction.

Daniil sits stiffly on the porch, his hands clenched in his lap. "If you're here to kill me," he starts, "please don't do it in front of my family."

I shake my head. "We're not here to kill you."

"We *were* going to kill you," Sasha adds bluntly, his eyes cold. "But the plan changed."

Daniil's expression remains grim. "I don't understand."

I lock eyes with him, my voice cool and calm as I lay it out. "We're the ones who killed your brother Dimitri."

Daniil's expression hardens into anger, and he sits up straighter. "Dimitri," he mutters, his jaw clenched. "I'm not happy about what happened to him, but I warned him. I told him not to cross the Bratva, not to steal from them. He didn't listen."

Sasha leans forward and says, "He paid the price."

Daniil's fists unclench slightly. His eyes flick to Sasha, an understanding passing between them. "Dimitri was reckless. Stupid, even. But he was still my brother." He glances toward the house where his wife and kids are. "All the same, I don't want to follow him to the grave."

I'm unmoved. "That's why we're here. It's not just about Dimitri. It involves your other brother, Denis. I need to find him."

Daniil looks genuinely confused, his brow furrowing. "Denis? What the hell does he have to do with this?"

Sasha and I exchange a glance. This is going to be more complicated than we thought.

"Denis and one of his associates broke into my house and tried to kill me. Held a gun to my woman's head. More than that, he's made it clear he's not giving up until she and I are dead."

Daniil's eyes flash with fury, his accent thickening as he spits out, "That fucking idiot!" His hands clench into fists again, and it's clear the weight of what his brother has done is sinking in. "He signed his own damn death warrant."

He shakes his head, frustration and anger mixing in his expression. "Denis came to me a while back, rambling about revenge for Dimitri. I told him he was being ridiculous, that going after the Bratva—let alone you—was suicidal. I didn't think he was serious. Hell, I thought he was just blowing off steam."

His voice tightens. "We got into it about Dimitri. Denis was obsessed with getting even and wanted me to help him. I told him no, that he was out of his goddamn mind. It got physical, and my wife nearly called the cops on us."

Daniil looks between Sasha and me, sadness in his eyes. "I'm out of that life; you have to believe me. I've been trying to leave it behind for years. My family… we're moving far away for a new start. I was hoping to get away from my maniac brother before something like this happened."

He's pleading now, but there's a deep sincerity in his voice. "I swear, I want nothing to do with this."

I can see in his eyes that he's telling the truth.

Daniil exhales sharply, running a hand through his slicked-back hair. "I told Denis straight up that if he went through with this, we were done. I've seen how it works. It's a never-ending fucking cycle."

His voice cracks slightly, but his resolve is clear. "I've watched enough families get caught in the crossfire, and I'll be damned if mine becomes one of them. Cutting ties with him is the hardest damn thing I've ever done. But I did it, no hesitation. I've got a wife and kids to think about."

He gestures toward the house again where his family is probably wondering if he's ever coming back inside. His voice drops, rough and raw. "That's all I want. To live in peace, to keep my family safe."

I say nothing, my mind processing his words, weighing the truth in them. I believe him. The anger in his eyes isn't for Sasha or me—it's for Denis. for the mess his brother has dragged him into. The man is desperate to escape this life, to keep his family out of harm's way. I can see that, and I can also respect it.

I glance at Sasha, and we share a look. It's clear we're thinking the same thing—Daniil is telling the truth. There's no deceit in his eyes, just exhaustion and desperation to protect his family.

But what Denis has done can't be undone.

"When are you leaving?"

"Tomorrow," he replies quickly. "It's moving day, actually."

I nod slowly, processing the information. "Good. Get far away from here. It's too late for your brother, but not for you. Get out while you still can."

Daniil's face tightens with relief, but I'm not finished. My tone turns colder, sharper. "But if you try to help Denis in any way—warn him, tip him off, anything..."

I let the threat hang in the air, unfinished. He knows what I'm saying.

Daniil's eyes widen, and he nods vigorously. "I won't. I swear I'm done. Just make it quick for him. Please." He says it as if he's almost pleading with me.

I study him for a moment, my gaze never leaving his. Then, without another word, I rise to my feet. Sasha stands beside me, his broad frame casting a shadow over the porch.

"Thank you," Daniil says, his voice thick with relief. "Thank you for sparing me."

I meet his eyes once more. "As long as you play this the smart way, you'll never see us again."

With that, we turn and walk away, leaving Daniil in the dim light of his porch, his future hanging on his next move.

We get back in the car, the engine rumbling to life as Sasha pulls away from the curb. I watch Daniil through the sideview mirror. He's moving slowly, like a man in a daze, his shoulders slumped, his whole world shaken.

Sasha breaks the silence. "We made the right call. And the guy's lucky as hell. Anyone else would've shot him on the spot just to send a message to his brother."

I nod slowly, staring out the window as the dark streets of Oakland pass by. "We don't kill like that. Never have."

Sasha grunts in agreement. The drive back to San Francisco is a quiet one. The city lights blur as my mind drifts, lost in the thought of what Daniil said about wanting peace, about cutting ties with his brother to keep his family safe.

Can I achieve the same? A peaceful life with Amelia? A family?

The idea has been gnawing at me ever since she came into my life. I've never wanted to settle down, never even considered it. But now I can't stop thinking about what it would be like. A life with her, a home, maybe even a child. But how realistic is that with the life I've lived? With the enemies I've made?

Daniil is right, the only way to keep them safe is to leave; uproot everything and start fresh somewhere far away.

Is that what I'm willing to do for her?

CHAPTER 32

MELOR

"It's almost Christmas."

Amelia's standing by the window, her fingers tracing the cold glass as she looks out at the neighborhood. The Christmas lights flicker in the distance, casting a faint glow across her face.

I don't respond, I just watch her. She's been restless, more so each day. I can tell she's getting tired of being cooped up in here, trapped for her own safety. I know she wants her life back the way it was before.

I get it. I don't want her to feel like a prisoner but what happens when it's finally safe for her to leave? What if she walks out of here and out of my life?

She told me she loves me. I want to believe it, but the reality is, when all this is over, she'll have the choice to go back to how things were. And maybe she'll want that more than staying here with me.

I watch her closely, thinking about how she's been acting lately. Distant. Preoccupied. Every time I ask if something's bothering her, she dodges the question, brushing it off with some lame excuse. It leaves me wondering if she's already planning her exit.

She finally turns from the window, her expression guarded. "I need a nap," she says, leaving the room before I can say anything else.

I watch her walk away, frustration building inside me. Something's wrong, and I don't know what it is. But I can feel her slipping away, and that's not something I'm willing to let happen. Not without a fight.

I don't have much time to dwell on Amelia's sudden distance before my phone rings. The screen lights up with a video call from Mashkov. I answer, taking the call in my office. His face appears, wind whipping through his silver hair, an endless stretch of blue water behind him. He's on a yacht.

I smirk. "Nice. Retirement suits you."

Mashkov grins, a cigar hanging from his lips. "You should try it sometime, Melor. The sea air, the freedom... no one trying to put a bullet in your head."

I chuckle. "Not in this life."

His grin fades, and he leans in closer to the camera. "Let's get to it. I've got Denis' location."

That gets my full attention. "Where?"

"East San Jose," Mashkov says, taking a drag from his cigar. "Sketchy part of town. He's staying with some woman—could be an ex, could be his current lover, hard to say."

"Doesn't matter who she is, Mashkov. What matters is getting Denis alone. I don't want her involved. If we can get him alone, fine. But if not, we keep her clear."

I end the call with Mashkov, my mind already working through the details. I message Sasha next, filling him in on everything. His response is immediate: *I'll be there when it's time. Just give the word.*

With everything set, I lean back in my chair, the weight of the plan settling over me. Duke jumps onto my lap, his soft fur brushing against my hand. He always seems to know when I've got something on my mind, his little motor kicking in as he nestles against me.

I scratch behind his ears, my thoughts swirling. We've got Denis' location, and we're close to finishing this. But I can't shake the feeling that once it's over, nothing will be the same.

I push the thought away. It doesn't matter right now. All that matters is ending this, taking Denis out, and securing our safety. Once he's gone, maybe I can finally have some peace with my woman.

But first, I've got to make sure there's a future to protect.

I hear footsteps rushing toward my office, quick and urgent. My muscles tense, expecting the worst, but when Amelia bursts into the room, her face isn't filled with fear, it's lit with pure joy.

"Claire's going into labor!" she exclaims, breathless. "We have to get to the hospital now!"

For a split second, I'm caught off guard, but then I smile. "We'll leave in a minute."

She's gone before I can say another word, hurrying upstairs to change. As soon as she's out of sight, I pull out my phone and text Sasha.

Claire's in labor. We're heading to the hospital. Meet us there and do a perimeter check with Mashkov's men.

Sasha's response is fast, as always.

On my way.

CHAPTER 33

AMELIA

I throw on my jacket and rush downstairs, practically tripping over my own feet.

Melor's already by the door, looking calm and collected, of course. Meanwhile, I'm buzzing with excitement. Duke is perched on a shelf in the hallway, watching us. I give him a quick scratch behind the ears.

"We'll be back," I tell him, like he's a little person who needs reassurance.

As soon as we step outside, Mashkov's men are there, approaching the house. One of them steps up and asks, "Heading out?"

Melor nods. "Her friend's in labor. We're going to the hospital."

"Need an escort?" the other guy asks, like we're heading into enemy territory instead of a maternity ward.

Before Melor has the chance to think about it I answer. "No."

Melor shoots me a look, one that clearly says *we're not discussing this here*. But I don't care. Claire's having a baby, and the last thing she needs is to see a couple of Russian bodyguards hovering around the hospital.

I can tell Melor wants to push back but after a long sigh he turns to the guys. "Keep an eye on the house while we're gone. And top off Duke's food and water."

The men nod, and I swear one of them smiles when they see Duke sitting there like he owns the place.

We jump in the car, but before we can pull out onto the street, a fancy sports car pulls up beside us, tires barely making a sound on the pavement. I tense up immediately, my heart thumping in my chest. "Who's that?"

Melor, totally unfazed, glances over. "That's Sasha."

I blink. "Sasha?"

"My close friend. The one I met in the middle of the night. He's coming with us."

I'm about to protest but Melor cuts me off. "It's a compromise. No hulking bodyguards, just my friend. He'll make sure things are safe, but he'll keep a low profile doing it."

I sigh, running my fingers through my hair. "Okay, but Claire *cannot* get stressed out. We're supposed to be supporting her, not turning her delivery room into an action movie set."

"He'll stay back. She won't even notice."

Sasha, a massive guy with a shaved head, expensive clothes, and flashy shoes, approaches the car. He taps on the window, and Melor rolls it down.

"Hop in," Melor tells him as he nods over his shoulder.

Sasha slides into the backseat, filling up the whole damn space with his presence. He looks at me. "Sasha," he says, grinning as if we're old friends. "You must be Amelia."

I'm a bit wary. This guy looks like he could pick me up with one hand. "Yeah. Nice to meet you."

We pull out onto the street, and Sasha leans forward between the seats like he's settling in for a casual road trip, not a potentially dangerous escort mission.

"So," he starts, "Melor tells me you've got yourself a kitten now. What's his name?"

"Duke."

Sasha chuckles. "Ah, a regal name. Fitting for Melor's place. I can already picture him lounging on one of those fancy couches like he owns the joint."

Melor glances at Sasha in the rearview mirror. "You're not far off."

"Smart cat," Sasha replies, his grin widening. "And I bet you're already wrapped around his little paw, huh?" He nudges Melor's seat playfully.

I can't help but laugh at the thought of Melor being bossed around by a kitten. "Wouldn't quite say that. But he's a nice addition."

Sasha shakes his head as he leans back in his seat. "Never thought I'd see the day. Melor, feared ex-Bratva badass, taking orders from a kitten."

Melor doesn't say a word, but I catch the tiniest smirk on his face.

As we drive, Sasha leans forward again, all casual and chatty. "You know," he says, grinning, "this VIP hospital visit is a total first for me. Usually, when Melor and I are heading somewhere, it's... let's just say, not about babies and kittens."

Melor raises an eyebrow, but doesn't say a word, eyes fixed on the road.

I snicker, and Sasha winks at me. "I gotta say, Amelia, it's kinda wild seeing my old buddy here doing something normal. When he first told me about you, I knew I had to meet the woman who's managed to make him less... well, less Melor. Do you know how rare that is?"

I glance at Melor, noticing how tightly he's gripping the steering wheel. I can tell he's not entirely comfortable with the conversation.

"Seriously, though," Sasha continues, smirking. "This guy's always been a solo act. Didn't think anyone could get through that concrete wall of his. But then you come along, and boom—now he's got a kitten, and he's playing house. You must be something special."

I feel my face heat up. "I don't know about that."

"Oh, don't even start," Sasha retorts, totally teasing. "I've known this guy for ages, and he doesn't keep people around for no reason. If he's holding onto you, it's because you knocked him flat on his ass."

Melor finally chimes in, voice low and serious. "She's done more than that."

Sasha bursts out laughing. "See? That's what I'm talking about! He's a goner, and honestly, I couldn't be happier."

I glance at Melor, half-expecting him to brush it off, but he doesn't. For a guy who's always kept his guard up, this is different in a good way.

Sasha slaps Melor's shoulder, clearly loving this. "Took you long enough, man. You deserve a good woman."

"And I've got one," Melor replies. Sasha leans back, eyes twinkling with that mischievous grin of his. "You know, I've got a story for you, Amelia. Picture this: Melor and me, back in the day, trying to be all serious and intimidating, right? But we were young and stupid. One night, we were supposed to meet this dude. And Melor here, tough guy that he is, decides to lead us through a shortcut."

I raise an eyebrow, already intrigued. "A shortcut?"

"Yep. Through someone's backyard. What he *didn't* know was that the yard belonged to an old lady with a massive Doberman."

I can't help but laugh at the mental image. "Oh no."

"Oh yes," Sasha continues, laughing. "The dog, Satan—and yes, that was its actual name—comes barreling out of nowhere. The always cool, calm, and collected Melor freaks out and starts scaling the fence like he's in the Olympics, leaving me behind to deal with the dog. Luckily, I had some beef jerky in my pocket, and I had to bribe it with that to stop it from eating me."

I glance over at Melor, who's shaking his head, clearly annoyed but also slightly amused. "It wasn't *that* bad."

"Not that bad?" Sasha scoffs. "I still have nightmares about that dog. And you just stood there, laughing from the other side of the fence once you were safe."

I burst out laughing. "I can't picture Melor running from a dog."

Sasha glances at me again, curiosity all over his face. "So, tell me more about this bakery of yours. Claire's your bestie, right? You two run the place together?"

I nod, smiling. "Yeah, it's called Sweet Talk. We make cupcakes, cookies, all the usual pastries but with a twist."

Sasha raises an eyebrow. "A twist, huh? Like what? You hiding something spicy in those cupcakes?"

I laugh. "No, no, although that's not a bad idea. We do fun flavors. Like, for Christmas, we have peppermint mocha cupcakes that are insanely good. They sell out quickly every year."

"Sounds dangerous," Sasha says, grinning. "You must have a cult following."

I shrug. "It's definitely picking up. Claire's got all these plans for expansion, too. We've been talking about opening up a second location."

Sasha gives me an impressed nod. "That's legit. You two sound like you've got it figured out. Is this her first kid?"

"Yes, and she's been a total trouper throughout her pregnancy. Still working up until last week. I don't know how she does it."

"Well, you'll have to bring me one of those cupcakes sometime. I'm a sucker for sweets." Sasha winks. "I'll even pay full price."

Melor, who's been quietly focused on driving, finally cuts in with a small smirk. "He's lying. He'll try to bargain you down for at least half off."

Sasha clutches his chest, mock offended. "Come on, man, I've got some dignity. Not a lot, but some."

As we pull into the hospital's underground parking garage, my laughter fades into nervous excitement. The reality of it hits me—Claire's about to have her baby. "This is really happening," I mumble, mostly to myself.

A noise catches my attention. I glance at the sideview mirror and see a car turning in behind us, but I immediately disregard it when my phone buzzes. It's a text from David.

"Contractions are getting closer," I read the message out loud. "They're thinking it's gonna be soon. Like, *really* soon."

Melor gives me a small smile. "I'll find a parking spot fast. We'll get there in time."

I can't help but wonder if he's going to be this calm when I'm the one in labor. The thought hits me like a freight train, and my stomach does a flip. I really need to tell him about this baby sooner than later.

We circle the garage, and I watch Melor scan for an open spot, still cool as a cucumber. Sasha cracks a joke from the back about how all hospital parking garages are mazes and I laugh, but my mind's wandering again.

Melor parks in a spot with no other cars around, and I'm practically bouncing in my seat, ready to jump out the second the wheels stop moving. I throw the door open, but before I can take a step, Melor's firm voice cuts through the air.

"Wait." He's already hurrying around the side of the car, but I'm so excited to get to Claire, I can barely stand still.

Out of the corner of my eye, I see the car I noticed earlier drive past us and stop a few spaces away. I frown, my instincts flaring. It's probably nothing but something about it sticks with me.

"What?" Melor asks, instantly picking up on my hesitation.

"I'm sure it's no big deal," I say, "but that car followed us into the garage."

Before I realize what's happening, the back doors of the car swing open, and two men step out. I freeze, eyes widening as I take in the guns pointed right at us.

"Get down!" Melor yells, his voice filled with an urgency I've never heard before.

Everything happens in a blur. I drop to the ground, my heart pounding in my chest as the unmistakable sound of gunfire rings out.

CHAPTER 34

MELOR

Gunshots ping off the steel of nearby cars, thudding into the concrete.

I keep my head low, instincts firing, my mind on the safety of Amelia and Sasha. I spot Sasha first, relief flooding through me. He's got Amelia on the ground, covering her, yelling at her to stay down and out of sight.

I draw my gun, cursing under my breath. I'm not as armed as I was at Daniil's—no submachine gun, no vest. Still, I've got enough, and I know Sasha's carrying.

Sasha's already drawn his weapon. Our eyes meet, and we both know what needs to happen.

I move quickly, crouching low, and make my way over to them. "You okay?" I ask Amelia.

"Yeah," she breathes, her eyes wide. "Should I call the police?"

"No." I shake my head, scanning the area. "Someone had to have heard those shots. They'll call. You just stay down."

Her face is pale, but she nods in understanding. I glance back at the car that the two assholes had jumped out from.

The gunfire pauses and I listen, an eerie silence fills the garage. Sasha leans in, his voice low. "They had one shot at this. They might be running for it now, realizing they fucked up."

I nod, still scanning the area. "Maybe. But I doubt it."

I start to get up, but Amelia grabs my arm, her eyes wide with fear. "We need to stay down," she hisses, her grip tight. "Wait for the police, for help."

I meet her gaze full-on. "No. I need to end this now. If I don't, they'll just keep coming. We'll never be free."

She releases me, her hand trembling. "Be careful," she pleads.

The look in my eyes is my silent promise to her. I have to take care of this. I can't let her live in fear any longer, not when I have the opportunity to stop it now.

A Russian-accented voice cuts through the garage. "Melor!"

It echoes off the concrete, filled with malice. I grip my gun tighter, rising from behind the car. I scan the rows of parked vehicles, my pulse steady, my mind sharp.

"Come out and face me!" the voice taunts. There's no doubt whom it belongs to.

I move carefully, every muscle tense.

"Denis!" I shout. "It's your lucky day. I'm in the mood to negotiate. After what you pulled, it's fair game, but if you leave the woman out of this, I'm willing to talk."

An amused laugh is his immediate response. "Negotiate? No, Melor, you're all going to die. But maybe I'll keep the girl and have a little fun with her first."

Rage ignites within me and my blood boils, pulsing hot and vicious. Any further thought of talking this down evaporates.

He's dead.

Gunshots crack through the air, and I instinctively duck behind a car, metal pinging as the bullets slam into the vehicles around us. Every nerve ending is coiled tight with fury. I squeeze the trigger, sending return fire into the garage, the echo of my shots roaring in my ears.

The gunfire is coming from two different positions. I can tell from the pattern of the shots they're working together, trying to box us in.

I grit my teeth, firing off some more suppressing shots before moving between cars. "Stay down!" I bark at Amelia, then signal to Sasha. We've done this dance before.

We'll take them out one by one. I've got no other option.

As I move, Denis' mocking laughter follows me like a shadow.

You won't be laughing much longer motherfucker.

"You're running out of time, Melor! Maybe I'll let you watch while I play with her."

A barrage of machine gun fire tears through the garage, the deafening roar of bullets ricocheting off metal and concrete.

I throw myself to the ground, glass shattering around me as I crawl between the cars, my gun ready in my hand. I hear the machine gun's magazine run dry and take my chance. I raise up and fire, aiming for Denis. But there's no clear shot.

A new gunshot comes from behind me. Shit. They've got us pinned.

Realization hits me—Denis' machine gun fire was a distraction while his companions maneuvered into a better position. I turn just in time to see him rise, aiming directly at Amelia.

Time slows. My heart pounds in my chest.

Before I can react, Sasha dives over her, shielding her body as I squeeze the trigger. The shooter ducks behind cover just in time, avoiding the shot. Fuck!

I grit my teeth, my blood boiling in my veins. I won't let them get near her. Not while I still breathe.

Machine gun fire erupts again, the deafening roar of bullets rattling throughout the parking garage. I hear Amelia let out a shriek and rage surges through me, hotter than anything I've felt before. My mind blanks, and instinct takes over. I rush toward Amelia and Sasha, barely processing the gunfire raining down around me. They're trying to pull the same move, using the machine gun to keep me pinned while the second guy lines up his shot.

Not this time.

I press myself against the cold steel of a nearby car, waiting for that brief pause when the machine gun runs dry again. The firing stops. I take a quick breath, steady my hand, and watch the second man rise, his weapon trained on Amelia and Sasha.

This time, I'm ready.

I let the air out of my lungs, sight in on him, and squeeze the trigger. The shot rings out, clean and sharp. The man's head snaps back, a neat hole drilled in his forehead. He drops to the ground, lifeless.

CHAPTER 35

AMELIA

Sasha's covering me like a shield, keeping me tucked down behind the car.

"Stay down, no matter what," he growls.

I hear Melor's footsteps, and I exhale a shaky breath. He's okay. At least for now.

"Are you alright?" I whisper to Sasha, my heart hammering in my chest.

"I'm fine," he grunts. His focus is sharp as he scans the garage. "But you better stay in one piece. Melor will kill me if anything happens to you."

Just then, something catches my eye—dark red—soaking through Sasha's shirt. My stomach twists.

"Sasha," I breathe, staring at the blood. "You've been shot."

His face is stone-like, but I see a flicker of pain in his eyes. "Don't worry about me. Focus on staying down and staying alive."

I swallow hard, feeling like I'm about to throw up, my heart clenching.

"You're gonna be okay," I say. "We're in a hospital parking lot."

Sasha laughs but it's weak. "I'm gonna be just fine," he says, but I can see the color draining from his face and I know that's not good.

My heart pounds in my chest, and I'm about to tell him he needs help when he reaches into his jacket and pulls out a gun, shoving it into my hands. I stare at it, frozen. "Just in case," he mutters, his voice strained.

"I don't know how to use this!" I declare. Guns aren't exactly my specialty.

He grins through the pain, coughing. Blood splatters onto his lips, and my stomach turns again. "It's simple," he says, "like a camera. Point and shoot. Safety's off."

Shit, shit, shit. My hands are trembling, the weight of the gun too real. This isn't a damn movie—this is life or death—and I don't know if I can do this.

Sasha coughs again, blood trickling from his mouth. His breathing's getting worse, shallow and ragged. I'm terrified he's going to die.

"Just stay alive," he murmurs, his voice barely above a whisper now. "And... take care of Melor. And your little kitten."

His eyes slowly close, and my blood turns to ice. Is he dead? I can't tell.

Panic claws at my chest.

Melor fires off a few more shots, each one ringing out in the garage like thunder. I strain to listen, my ears picking up on the silence from the gun that was firing rapid bursts earlier.

Then, I hear Melor's voice, strong and commanding. "Denis, I can tell you're out of ammo. You're alone, and more or less unarmed. Good time to surrender, don't you think?"

A laugh echoes back, wild and unhinged. "You think that's the only gun I have? Try me!" Denis' voice sounds feral; he's out of control.

I press my fingers to Sasha's neck, checking his pulse. It's faint, and the blood pooling beneath him is spreading fast.

No, no, no!

My mind's racing. He's bleeding out, and I have no clue how to help him.

An evil laugh pulls my focus away from Sasha. I whip my head around, heart slamming into my chest.

It's Denis. He's found me.

A gun gleams in his hand, aimed right at my head, a wild, crazed look in his eyes.

My breath catches.

This is it.

"Hey there, sweetheart," he sneers. My entire body freezes, fear locking me in place.

I want to scream for Melor. but I am unable to speak. All I can do is stare down the barrel of Denis' gun, praying for a miracle.

Another shot rings out.

Melor's behind me, taking aim at Denis again. Relief surges through me, but it's short-lived. Denis manages to fire back before Melor can get another shot off. The sound of the gunshot rips through the air, and Melor stumbles back, his body jerking from the impact.

I scream. Without thinking, I bolt toward him, my feet moving faster than my brain can keep up. I dive behind the nearby car where Melor's crouched, clutching his shoulder. Blood stains his shirt, and his face twists in pain.

"Fuck," he hisses through gritted teeth, clearly pissed he got shot. His eyes flash with fury and I can feel the rage radiating off of him. I look down at my trembling hands and realize I'm still holding the gun Sasha gave me.

"Melor," I whisper, my voice shaky.

He glances at me, his eyes fierce but soft. "I'm fine. It's just a graze," he lies. "But you need to get out of here. I'm going to create a distraction, and you're going to run. Got it?"

"No way," I snap, shaking my head. "I'm not leaving you."

Denis' voice cuts through the air, dripping with sadistic glee. "You two lovebirds hiding back there? Come on out! I'll make it quick... after I'm done with your little girlfriend!"

"Get ready," Melor growls, eyes locked on mine.

The footsteps get closer, heavy and deliberate. Melor pulls me close, his body tense. I try to help him to his feet, but he's too heavy, his weight pressing against me. Blood spreads across his shirt, soaking through. I know it's bad and my heart is breaking.

Finally, Denis steps into view, his gun aimed right at Melor.

I tuck Sasha's gun away, hoping Denis doesn't see it.

Denis smirks, his eyes gleaming with twisted satisfaction. "Drop the gun, or I kill the girl." He jabs the barrel toward me for emphasis.

Melor's jaw tightens, and with a glare that could melt steel, he slowly lowers his weapon, his eyes never leaving Denis. I can see the pain in his face, both from the gunshot and the fact that he's being forced to submit.

Denis' grin widens. "Revenge for my brother. Justice, at last."

Melor scoffs, blood trickling down his arm. "There's no justice here, you piece of shit. You've just signed your own death warrant."

"Whatever," Denis shrugs, taking a step closer, his gun still trained on Melor. "At least I'll be satisfied."

I pull the gun out from behind me, raise it, and before I can overthink, I fire.

The shot goes wide, hitting a pipe on the ceiling behind Denis with a loud clang.

Denis flinches, whipping his head around in confusion. "What the fuck?" he says, his eyes narrowing. I've spoiled his little villain moment. But that split second of distraction is all Melor needs.

In a blur of motion, Melor grabs his gun, raises it, and fires. Bang, bang. Two clean shots—one straight to the head, one to the chest. Denis doesn't have time to process what's happening before he collapses to the ground, dead.

I stand there, frozen, my heart pounding in my throat.

Melor scans me from head to toe. "You okay?"

I nod, but my mind's elsewhere. "Sasha," I manage to choke out, pointing to where Sasha had fallen. "He was shot."

Together, we hurry over, my stomach twisting in knots. Melor kneels beside his friend, his fingers searching for a pulse. The seconds stretch on forever, and I hold my breath, praying for a miracle.

Melor's face falls, his hand dropping back to his side. "He's dead."

CHAPTER 36

AMELIA

I lower my phone, Claire's text lighting up the screen: *The baby's here!* It's followed by a picture of her in the hospital bed, holding the cutest little boy I've ever seen. He looks so perfect, so peaceful. My heart squeezes, half because I'm so happy for her and half because I'm shaken beyond belief.

Red and blue police lights flash around me, blending with the insanity of everything that just went down. I'm standing outside the parking garage, surrounded by cops. They're busy taking statements and combing through the scene.

Melor's beside me, calm as ever, but I can feel the tension rolling off him. He leans in close, "You remember the story?"

I nod, repeating it in my head like a TikTok script. "We parked, got out of the car, then we were ambushed. We didn't see anything. We weren't involved. Just innocent bystanders."

It feels horrible, lying like this. I hate it. But what choice do I have? I push down the rising nausea, glancing at the stretcher where they're loading Sasha's body bag into the van. I can't believe he's actually gone.

I glance at Melor. His face is totally unreadable, his emotions locked down tight.

I grip my phone harder, the picture of Claire holding her baby blurring as my eyes fill with tears.

"I feel bad lying about Sasha, acting like he was some random guy when he literally saved our lives," I say, staring at the ground. It's eating me up inside, knowing the truth and not being able to tell anyone. Sasha was more than just a guy caught in the crossfire.

Melor nods, his jaw clenched. "I get it. But it's the only way out of this." He says it so calmly, like he's already accepted what we have to do. "I checked the garage—no cameras. We wiped the guns clean. There's nothing to tie us to the shooting." He pauses, his eyes darkening. "Sasha would want it this way. He wouldn't want us to pay for what happened."

I nod, biting my lip. He's probably right. But it still feels so wrong. Sasha was his friend, and it feels like we're just erasing him. The pit in my stomach gets deeper, and I quickly grab my phone, texting Claire back.

I'll be up ASAP.

As soon as I hit send, my chest tightens. How am I supposed to walk into that hospital room, see Claire holding her brand-new baby boy and act like *this* didn't just happen?

I glance over at Melor. He's keeping it together, but I can tell he's carrying the weight of it all. "What the hell am I supposed to tell Claire?" I whisper, feeling the tears building up again.

Melor squeezes my hand. "We'll figure that out later," he says. "No need to worry a new mother with what just happened. The important thing is that we're safe now. Denis is dead, and the threat's over."

His words begin to settle in but my mind's still buzzing. My eyes drift to the hospital's Christmas decorations—twinkling lights, garland, ornaments, and tinsel everywhere. It feels surreal being surrounded by so much cheer after staring death in the face.

Without thinking, I blurt, "Your place isn't Christmassy at all, you know."

He looks at me, confusion clouding his face, probably wondering why the hell I'm thinking about Christmas decor right now.

"We need to fix that," I continue. "Get a tree, hang some lights, maybe a wreath on the door. We don't have much time—it's only a week or so until Christmas."

He raises an eyebrow, smirking. "So does that mean you want to stay with me?"

I feel a blush creeping up my cheeks. I meet his gaze and smile. "Yeah, I do. I'm ready for whatever's next with you. Hell, it can't be any worse than this."

His expression softens as he pulls me closer, planting a kiss on my forehead. It's crazy, after everything that just happened—guns, blood, and lies—I still feel so safe with him.

The detectives approach, and Melor and I give them the story I've rehearsed in my head a hundred times. We describe what happened, both of us cool as cucumbers. He's clearly wearing off on me. I can tell from their faces that they're not buying it completely, but after a few more questions, they finally leave. As soon as they're out of earshot, I turn to Melor.

"You think we're good?"

He nods once. "We're clear."

I let out a breath I didn't realize I was holding and text Claire, telling her I'm ready to see the baby. She immediately replies, telling me to get my butt up there now. I smile, the anxiety slowly draining from my body as we head inside the hospital.

When we step into the room, everything else fades away. Claire's lying in bed, glowing like she's never been more alive. David's standing next to her, beaming down at the tiny bundle in her arms. The world outside, the chaos downstairs, ceases to exist.

"Meet William," David says, his voice full of pride as he introduces their baby boy. I lean over, peeking at his little face, so peaceful and perfect.

Claire looks up at me, her face glowing with pure joy. In that moment, I can't help but marvel at how beautiful life can be, how it just keeps going.

CHAPTER 37

MELOR

I step back from the front of the house and dust off my hands, taking in the final result.

The lights are strung up, the wreaths are set, and everything is in place. It's Christmas Eve, and even though it took longer than I'd planned to get things right, the house finally looks ready for the holidays.

"Better late than never," Amelia says at my side, adding a teasing wink. I glance down at her, bundled up against the cold. She's watching me closely, her breath visible in the sharp air.

"It's cold," she mutters, rubbing her hands together, her eyes sweeping across the street to her house.

The "For Sale" sign glares back at us. I've been thinking, and I can't help but offer, "If you miss it, you could keep it as a private writing space."

She looks back at me, shaking her head slightly. "No, I like the room upstairs just fine." She pauses, then adds with a sly smile, "And my roommate's not so bad either."

There's a light in her eyes that makes my chest tighten. I take a step closer. We're about to kiss, the cold air between us practically sizzling, when her phone buzzes. She grins, her breath fogging the air as she pulls back slightly. "It's Claire, about dinner tomorrow."

I turn my attention back to the house, taking in the lights strung up along the roof, the wreath on the door. The place finally feels like Christmas, something I haven't bothered with in years. But for her, it's worth the effort.

"There might even be snow tonight," I say.

She looks up at me, surprised. "A white Christmas? Here?"

"White for this part of the world," I reply. "A light dusting maybe. But it's better than nothing."

She chuckles. "I'll take it."

I glance at her, catching the way she's still focused on her phone. I tell myself not to read too much into it, but then a thought crosses my mind. "Next year, let's go somewhere with a lot of snow for the holidays," I suggest, picturing us somewhere remote, where the snow falls heavy and silent.

Her expression falters, just for a second, and a flicker of what looks like uncertainty takes over. It's gone as quickly as it came, replaced by her familiar smile. "That could be nice," she says, her voice warm but distant, like she's thinking about something else entirely.

"Let's go inside," she suggests, slipping her phone back into her pocket, the lost moment between us still lingering.

The house feels like a different place. Warm. Alive. Amelia had free rein to decorate, and she went all out. Twinkling lights of garland wrap around the banister, and a towering tree stands in the corner, loaded with ornaments that make the space feel both festive and personal.

Duke is curled up in front of the crackling fire, lost in a Christmas slumber, perhaps dreaming of catnip balls and play mice. Gifts are piled under the tree, wrapped in Amelia's bright, quirky style—nothing matches, but it all comes together somehow.

There's a smell of something hearty and festive in the air, drawing me toward the kitchen. I lift the lid on the roasting pan, catching the rich aroma of honey-glazed ham with rosemary and cloves. Alongside it, mashed potatoes and roasted vegetables are warming in the oven. It's a perfect Christmas dinner—something else I hadn't bothered with in years.

Amelia follows, her phone in hand. She taps the screen, and soon the kitchen fills with the sound of Christmas music.

"Frank Sinatra?" I ask with a smirk.

"My dad's favorite. I like to play it every year and think of him on Christmas morning belting it out with the Santa hat on."

I chuckle at the mental image.

She smiles, leaning against the counter. "Claire and David are all set for Christmas dinner tomorrow," she says.

"How's William?" I ask, stirring the soup as I glance her way.

"Freaking adorable," she replies, eyes bright with affection. "Seriously, he's baby model material."

I watch her as she moves around the kitchen, humming along to the music. There's something about this moment—the warmth, the normalcy—that makes me want to hold onto it forever.

I pour two glasses of wine and slide one over to her, but the moment her eyes land on it, something shifts. She hesitates, then, with a small smile, says, "Sparkling water's fine."

I narrow my eyes. "You sure you're okay?"

She brushes it off with a light laugh, but there's tension behind it. "Yeah, just want to be sharp for Christmas morning."

I don't buy it, but I let it slide—for now.

Her face suddenly changes, turning serious. She looks at the counter, avoiding my eyes. "I don't want to push but... Sasha."

"I'm still processing," I say, my voice tight. "The funeral's next week."

My hands grip the edge of the counter, tension building in my shoulders. She steps closer, her hand sliding over mine, grounding me in a way I didn't expect.

"You don't have to go through this alone," she says, voice soft but steady. "I'm here for you. Just don't forget that, okay?"

I nod, still not looking her way but I feel her words settling deep inside.

"He was loyal," I say quietly. "To the end."

I feel a tightness in my throat, the kind that makes it hard to breathe. I swallow it down, forcing myself to stay composed, but it doesn't make the ache go away. Amelia squeezes my hand gently, her eyes searching mine.

"I've had to cut ties before. It's part of the lifestyle—walking away when you need to. Friends, family. Sasha was one of the last of those ties I had left."

She watches me, her expression soft. "We can keep him alive in our memories."

"I'd like that."

She gives me a small smile, and it's like she knows exactly what I need to hear. "Our life together," she continues, "can be the opposite of your old one. We'll build new ties with friends and family. We'll put down roots."

I look at her, really look at her, and in that moment, she's more beautiful than I've ever seen her. There's something about the way she speaks, the way she's always so damn sure of what we could have, that makes me believe it, too. She's offering me something I never thought was possible. Stability. A future. Love.

I squeeze her hand back, a smile tugging at the corner of my mouth.

Dinner's ready, and I plate it up, the rich aroma filling the kitchen. Not bad, if I say so myself. Amelia's already at the table, and I bring over the dishes, setting them down. She looks up at me, her eyes full of warmth and love.

I raise my glass. "To Sasha," I say. "To his memory. And to always keeping it alive."

She lifts her own glass, smiling softly. "To Sasha. We'll never forget him."

We clink glasses, the sound small but solid, an unspoken promise. We each take a sip, then dig in. The food is good, but it's the moment itself that I'm savoring most. Amelia sitting across from me, this life we're building. I never thought I'd want something like this, but here we are, and I realize it's all I *ever* wanted.

As we eat, I bring up an idea that's been rolling around in my head. "I was thinking, once things settle down, when you can get some time away from work, we should take a trip. January, maybe. Clear our heads, reset, truly relax."

She brightens at that, nodding. "That could work. January's usually the slowest time of the year at the bakery, and Claire's been talking about taking a little maternity break. We could shut down for a week. I could brainstorm some new pastry ideas."

I smile. "I like the sound of that."

After dinner, we clean up with more kissing than actual scrubbing. As I towel off a dish, Amelia sneaks up behind me, wrapping her arms around my waist and pressing a kiss to my back. I turn, planting a kiss on her forehead. We laugh our way through the rest of it.

In the den, Duke's still curled up in front of the fire, the little guy owning the spot like a king. A crackling warmth fills the room, and sure enough, just like they predicted, a bit of snow starts to fall outside. I joke. "Better call the snowplows. Could be a real mess out there."

She snorts out a laugh, rolling her eyes. "Yeah, all two millimeters of it."

All the same, we both glance out at the light dusting—there's something so peaceful about it. I sip my wine and lean back on the couch, noticing again how she's sticking with sparkling water.

We sit curled up together, watching the fire, the soft glow of the Christmas tree bathing the room in warmth. Everything about this feels right; it's a moment I never thought I'd have but now don't ever want to lose. I look at her, her head resting on my chest. "I love you," I say quietly.

She tilts her head up, eyes soft, and whispers, "I love you, too."

Then, suddenly her eyes light up, like something just clicked. She shifts in my arms, her face serious but excited. "Melor, there's something I need to tell you."

I sit up a little straighter, the tightness in my chest back again. "What is it?" I ask. I'm bracing for something that could ruin this peace. I hate admitting it, but I can't shake the feeling.

She gives me a soft smile, one that doesn't quite ease the tension inside me. "I want to tell you, but... it's better if I show you."

Before I can respond, she's off the couch, rushing out of the room.

When she returns, she's holding a small gift, her eyes sparkling with something I can't quite place. She sits back down next to me, pressing the wrapped box into my hands, her expression nervous but excited.

"This moment with you is perfect," she says softly, "but there's something that could make it even better."

My heart skips a beat. How the hell is that possible? I glance down at the gift, then back at her. "What is it?"

She bites her lip. "I wanted to wait until tomorrow morning, but there's no way I can."

I raise an eyebrow, curiosity gnawing away at me. I can tell by the way her hands are shaking that it's something big. Slowly, I begin to peel back the wrapping paper, my eyes flicking to hers every second. Whatever this is, it's got her on edge, and now, I'm right there with her.

I tear the wrapping paper away, revealing a small, simple box. At first, it doesn't register. Then I see it—the pregnancy test, with a little pink plus sign staring back at me.

I hold it in my hands, still as a stone, the reality of it slowly sinking in.

A baby.

The silence stretches between us, thick and heavy. I can feel her eyes on me, waiting. Finally, she breaks the quiet, her voice shaky.

"Say something, anything. Even if you're upset." She's rambling, clearly nervous. "I know things are happening fast between us, and a baby wasn't in the plan, but I'm happy. I really am. And I think you'd be a great dad, but if you don't want to be involved, I get it. I can—"

I turn to her, stopping her words with a kiss, deep and full of everything I can't quite say yet. She melts against me, her body trembling slightly. I pull away slowly, my forehead resting against hers, my hand still clutching the test.

"It's the best news I've ever gotten," I whisper.

Her eyes fill with tears, her lower lip trembling. "Really?"

I nod, wiping away one of the tears that escapes down her cheek. "I love you, Amelia. I'm not going anywhere."

She smiles, and it's the most beautiful thing I've ever seen. "I love you, too."

I kiss her again, then pull back, grinning. "Let's head upstairs and celebrate the news properly."

EPILOGUE I

AMELIA

I stand in my chambers, my hand resting on the swell of my belly.

It's been three months since the duke was killed in battle, since I learned I was carrying his child.

The baby is growing, big and strong, and though the thought of becoming a mother fills me with joy, it's overshadowed by the unrelenting grief of losing my love. My heart aches for him more and more each day. It feels as though the castle itself is mourning his absence—cold and empty, despite its grandeur.

A sharp knock at the door pulls me from my reverie. I already know who it is before I answer.

Count Blackmoor.

He steps inside, tall and imposing, his sharp features framed by dark, shoulder-length hair. His eyes are cunning—a predator sizing up his prey. There's no doubt he's handsome but there's something deeply unsettling about him. His smile never quite reaches his eyes, and I can sense the malevolence behind every word.

"My lady," he says smoothly, his voice like silk. "How are you faring today?" His tone drips with false concern.

I narrow my eyes; I know exactly what game he's playing. With the duke gone, Count Blackmoor is next in line to inherit the estate, and by his calculations, he hopes to win my hand in marriage as part of the bargain.

"I'm managing," I reply cooly, though my heart races with unease.

His eyes flicker down to my belly, his smile widening ever so slightly. I've been able to hide my condition up to this point with loose-fitting clothing, but rumors are already swirling, and soon the secret of my pregnancy will be the talk of the estate.

"I'm sure you do."

He steps further into the room, his polished boots soundless against the stone floor. He makes himself comfortable, uninvited, on the edge of my bed. I tense at the sight, my fingers instinctively pressing against my belly as if to shield the life growing inside.

"My lady," he begins, his voice calculating, "I understand the grief that has consumed you in the wake of the duke's passing. You are in a... delicate state, and it is only natural to feel overwhelmed."

I bite my lip, refusing to give him the satisfaction of seeing how much his words sting. He knows nothing of my grief, only the opportunity it presents.

"But," he continues, leaning in slightly, his dark eyes glinting, "you must think practically. You are pregnant, and the eyes of the kingdom are upon you. There is a certain... expectation for how you must conduct yourself, especially now. I'm offering you a way out, a solution." He smiles, the expression as cold as winter. "Marry me, and I will ensure the safety of your child. We can silence any whispers of scandal. I will look after you both."

His words coil around me like a serpent. I know Count Blackmoor well enough to understand that his offer of protection is a farce. He'd find a way to eliminate my child, the duke's heir, the moment he could. He's not a man to leave loose ends—especially not when it involves a threat to his inheritance.

I refuse his proposal.

Count Blackmoor's face darkens at my rejection, though he tries to mask his frustration with a twisted smile. He's tried this before—this false charm, this sick game of making me believe I have a choice.

"You've always been insistent," I say, my voice cold. "But the answer is no. I would sooner raise my child as a bastard than submit to you."

The mask slips. His smile vanishes, replaced with simmering rage. He rises abruptly, crossing the room in swift strides and grabbing my arm. His grip is firm, and I can feel it bruising.

"You'd do well to watch your tongue," he growls, his face inches from mine. "I've been patient, offering you some sense of control in this. But make no mistake, you will be mine, whether you like it or not."

I yank my arm from his grasp, my heart racing, but I refuse to back down. "Never," *I hiss.* "I'd throw myself from this tower before I let you touch me."

He steps back, his lips curling into a snarl. "You're being a fool. The duke never loved you, not truly. He only wanted you for your body. But I, my lady," *he leans in, his voice low and threatening,* "I want all of you. And I will give you everything—power, wealth, security—if you just say yes. Marry me, and everything you've ever wanted is yours."

His eyes flash with something dark, something final as he says, "This is the last time I'm asking."

"No," *I say firmly, staring him down.* "And that is my final answer."

Count Blackmoor's eyes narrow, his jaw tightening. For a split second, I wonder if he'll lash out, if his rage will get the better of him.

His lips curl into a sinister grin, one that sends a chill down my spine.

"Don't underestimate me, my lady," *he warns.* "I'm capable of more cruelty than you could ever imagine."

"Like what?" *I ask defiantly despite the icy fear creeping through me.*

His evil grin widens. "It wasn't the enemy that killed your precious duke on the battlefield, you know. That was all me."

"What?" *My breath catches in my throat, my heart pounding.*

I'm stunned. My mind races, reeling from the horror of what he's just confessed. Without thinking, my hand flies across his face, the sound of the slap echoing through the room.

His eyes blaze with fury, and for a moment, I fear what he might do. His hand rises, but before he can strike, the sound of a throat clearing comes from the doorway.

We both freeze, turning to see none other than the duke himself.

He's alive.

Bruised, battered, but very much alive.

I blink, thinking I must be seeing things.

The duke steps into the room, his figure tall and commanding, and my heart soars—it's really him.

The count, pale with shock, stumbles backward. "How are you here?"

The duke's voice is calm, but there's a hard edge to it. "Considering your life as you know it is over, cousin," *he says, stepping closer,* "I suppose I'll give you an explanation."

I see the tension in the count's posture as the duke continues. "The rogues you hired tried to kill me, but they failed. Every last one of them fell by my sword." *He smirks, a dangerous glint in his eye.* "You should've hired better trained men."

The count's expression turns to one of defeat. "I—I—"

"I'll give you a sporting chance," *the duke interrupts,* "a head start to run. But know this—I will track you down." *His eyes flash with cold fury.* "And when I do, you'll wish those rogues had finished the job."

Stunned and terrified, the count stammers, then bolts from the room without another word.

The moment we're alone, the duke turns to me, his expression softening as he takes my hand. "I'm sorry," he says, his voice filled with sincerity. "I was wounded in the melee and had to lay low while I recovered."

Tears of relief well in my eyes as I grip his hand. "I'm so glad you're alive."

He kisses my hand tenderly. "I received news of our child," he says, his voice full of happiness and love. "And now, I'm ready to do what I should've done long ago, and that is, marry you."

We kiss, the words we've both been holding back finally spilling out between us.

"I love you."

"And I you, my lady. And I will forevermore."

∽

I sit up from my laptop, stretching my arms over my head. Another gorgeous day in San Francisco spills through the windows of my cozy little writing room. The sunlight bounces off the city below, making everything look like a postcard. I glance down at my big, pregnant belly with a smile. Three weeks until this little one arrives, and I'm determined to finish my book before then. It's practically writing itself at this point, but I still have to wrap it up with a cute happily ever after.

My phone buzzes, pulling me out of my thoughts. It's a text from Claire. I grin as I open it, a picture of her and William greeting me. He's growing like a weed, holding up a stuffed reindeer. Too cute.

Park later? she asks, complete with a heart emoji and a little stroller gif.

I chuckle, rubbing my belly as I type back.

I hit send and smile, loving that life's finally slowed down a bit. Things have been weirdly perfect lately even though Melor's still intense and protective. He's also still calm and grounding, and all of it is nice.

I start to stand when I feel a strange pop, wetness trailing down my leg.

"Melor!" I shout, trying to stay calm but definitely not succeeding.

Within seconds he's there, rushing through the door from his office like some kind of action hero.

"What is it?" he asks, voice filled with concern.

"My water just broke," I reply, half laughing, half panicking. "I think this baby's coming early."

His eyes widen, but he doesn't miss a beat. "Let's get you to the hospital."

And just like that, we're on the move.

"Overnight bags?" he calls, already halfway down the hall.

"By the door!" I shout back, waddling out of my writing room as fast as I can.

"Hospital forms? ID? Phone charger?" he fires off, grabbing stuff along the way.

"I think—wait, I didn't even know we had forms," I mutter, frantically checking my pockets for my phone.

He's already on his phone with the hospital as I'm slipping on my shoes. I shoot a quick text to Claire.

Water broke. Heading to the hospital!

Her reply comes instantly, all cap.

OMG SO EXCITING! KEEP ME POSTED!

We pile into the car, and as we pull out of the driveway, I steal a quick glance at my old house across the street. A new girl moved in a few months ago and is sitting on the stoop, earbuds in, scrolling through her phone. She's young, probably just getting her life started. I feel a weird pang of nostalgia, remembering when that was me.

But I wouldn't trade my life now for anything. Not for a second.

Melor speeds toward the hospital, and soon we're pulling up to the entrance. My heart's pounding, but it's not just nerves, it's excitement, too. We're about to meet our baby.

We rush through the hospital doors, everything flying by in a total blur. The contractions are getting closer and closer together, and I'm fairly sure time doesn't even exist anymore. Just pain, breathing, and Melor at my side. His hand never leaves my shoulder, always there grounding me, while the doctors do their thing.

We decided to keep the baby's gender a surprise, and even though I know I'll love this little bean no matter what, the curiosity is killing me.

I don't even remember getting into the delivery room or changing into a gown but the next thing I know I'm hearing the doctor say, "Push."

And suddenly, it happens. I feel the release, and I hear the baby's first cry. My heart swells like it's going to burst.

"It's a boy!" the nurse announces, placing him on my chest.

A boy. My beautiful, perfect baby boy.

I look down at him, this tiny human we made together, and I fall in love so hard it's like nothing I've ever felt before. His little fingers curl around mine, and I'm done, completely wrecked in the best way possible.

Melor leans over, kissing the top of my head, then looks down at his son, the love in his eyes unmistakable.

"Hey, little guy," I whisper, tears streaming down my face. "Welcome to the world."

We spend some blissful alone time fawning over our little guy. He's perfect. I can't stop staring at his tiny nose and his little fingers wrapped around mine. It's like I've known him my whole life. One of the nurses takes him for a quick clean-up, weigh-in, and testing, and as we watch from the bed, Melor and I chat.

"So, I know we had both boy and girl names picked out already, but I've been thinking."

He raises an eyebrow. "Oh? What's on your mind?"

I bite my lip, suddenly nervous to tell him. "I've been meaning to ask you this for a while, but I didn't know how you'd feel about it."

He shifts closer, his full attention on me now. "Go on."

I take a deep breath. "How would you feel about naming him Sasha?"

The look on his face stops my heart for a second. Melor's not a man who cries, like ever, but I can tell my words hit him right in the chest. He swallows hard, taking my hand and squeezing it tight.

"That's a great idea," he says, his voice softer than I've ever heard it. "I love it."

When the nurse brings our baby back, it's Dad's turn to hold him. I watch as Melor cradles little Sasha in his arms, his big, strong hands so gentle with this tiny new life. My heart feels like it's going to burst from all the love that is filling me.

EPILOUGE II

MELOR

December, two years later...

It's a quiet, rainy morning in San Francisco, the kind where the world feels like it's taking a little longer to wake up. I open my eyes and glance over at Amelia, still sound asleep beside me. Every morning with her feels like a gift I don't deserve, wrapped up in the peaceful rise and fall of her chest. I lie there for a while, taking her in—her soft breathing, the way her hair falls across her pillow.

I still can't believe she's mine.

After a few minutes she stirs, blinking her eyes open and turning to me with a sleepy smile.

"Morning," she murmurs, her voice hushed and intimate, like we're the only two people in the world.

"Morning."

She pauses, tilting her head slightly, listening. I raise an eyebrow. "What is it?"

"You hear that?" she asks.

I frown, straining my ears. "Hear what?"

A sly smile spreads across her lips. "Nothing. *Silence.* Sasha's still sleeping."

I chuckle, realizing where this is going. "So... you thinking what I'm thinking?"

She grins wider. "Hell, yes."

I close the distance between us, pulling her into a slow, deep kiss. There's nothing better than this—her naked warmth against me, the rain tapping against the window, the quiet of the morning stretching out before us. For once, no interruptions, just us.

I kiss her slowly at first, savoring the taste of her lips, the warmth of her body pressed against mine. Every inch of her is perfection, and I can't help but move my hands over her curves, pulling her closer, feeling the softness of her skin. She's wearing nothing more than a thin camisole and thong, and I waste no time slipping my hand under the hem of her top, gliding up her stomach until I'm cupping her breast.

She lets out a soft sigh into my mouth as I tug the fabric of her cami up and over her head, tossing it aside without a second thought. My other hand moves lower, tugging her thong down her legs. She's already soaked, and I groan, feeling her slick heat as my fingers dip between her thighs, teasing her, rubbing her just the way she likes.

"God, you're so perfect," I whisper against her lips.

She grins against my mouth, biting my lower lip as her hand slides down into my pajama pants, wrapping around my length. "I could say the same thing about you," she teases, her voice hushed and breathy.

Her touch is enough to drive me mad, stroking me as our bodies press together, my fingers moving in rhythm with her hand. I can tell she's getting close, her breath quickening, her hips rocking into my hand.

"Come for me," I whisper, my lips brushing her ear. "I want to feel you lose it." Her moan says everything.

I pull the covers down, just enough to take in the sight of her. She's always been beautiful, but now, after everything we've been through, after becoming a mother, she's somehow even more breathtaking. Her curves, her skin, the way her body responds to my touch—it's all perfect. I'm the luckiest man alive, and I know it.

I keep my fingers between her thighs, rubbing her just the way I know she needs. Her hips buck, her breath coming faster, until finally, she falls apart for me. She comes hard, her body trembling against mine, moaning my name like it's the only thing she can say. God, I love hearing her like that.

Before she can catch her breath, I pull her into me, spooning her. I'm rock hard and ready, slipping inside her with one smooth thrust, feeling her tight and warm around me. I groan, kissing her neck, her shoulder, every part of her I can reach.

She looks so incredibly sexy with her hair tousled, lips parted, and skin flushed. "You feel too good," I whisper against her ear, thrusting deeper. "How am I supposed to keep my hands off you?"

"Who said you had to?"

I kiss her again, gripping her hips as I move in and out, savoring every bit of her. I thrust in and out hard, watching as our bodies collide. The sight of her perfect ass against me, the way she reaches back and grips me tight, is enough to drive me crazy. Her moans fill the room, and I love the way she sounds—how she can't hold back, how she gives herself to me completely.

Her body tenses, her back arches, and I feel her pulse around me as she comes, gasping my name. I'm right there with her, on the edge, nearly ready to finish, but I'm not done with her yet.

As her orgasm fades, I pull out just long enough to move her onto her back. I climb over her, and the sight of her beneath me nearly takes my breath away. She's stunning—her chest rising and falling, her cheeks flushed with heat, her lips parted in that way that drives me wild. I'll never get tired of seeing her like this.

"I love you."

"I love you, too," she replies, her eyes locked on mine.

I slip back inside her, deep and slow, feeling her warmth wrap around me. We kiss, soft and sweet at first, then deeper, more intense, as I start to thrust again. Her legs wrap around me, pulling me closer, and we move together, perfectly in sync. We've become one, lost in each other, in the heat of our love.

I've got her right on the edge, her breath catching in her throat. She grips my shoulders, pulling me closer, and I can feel her need, her urgency.

"Come with me," she whispers, her eyes locking onto mine.

"You're a bossy one, aren't you?"

"You love it," she fires back, flashing me that playful grin that drives me insane.

"Damn right I do." I growl, thrusting harder, deeper, feeling her tighten around me.

A few more powerful thrusts, and I've got her right there, teetering on the brink. I watch as her body tenses, as she falls over the edge, her back arching, her moans filling the room. I follow, my body giving in and letting go as I come hard, filling her completely. The intensity hits me like a tidal wave, overwhelming, unstoppable.

We lay there in the afterglow catching our breath, and I pull her close, kissing her gently, taking in the moment. Her body against mine, the peace of the morning wrapping around us like a cocoon.

That is, until the peace is shattered. Sasha's voice crackles through the baby monitor.

"Mama! Dada!"

Amelia laughs softly, shaking her head. "So much for our quiet morning."

I can't help but laugh, too. I press a kiss to her forehead, reluctant to move but knowing we have to. "Guess that's our cue."

We untangle ourselves and get out of bed. Even with the interruptions, the noise, the chaos... I wouldn't trade this life for anything.

"Take your time getting ready," I tell her. "I'll get Sasha started with breakfast."

She rewards me with a soft kiss on the lips. "You'd better still have some gas in the tank later after he's down for the night," she says with a grin.

I smirk. "Always." She disappears into the bathroom, and I throw on some jeans and a T-shirt before heading to Sasha's room.

The little man's standing at the side of his crib, wailing his head off. "Alright, alright," I murmur, scooping him up. I can't help but smile. He's getting so big; it's hard to believe how fast time has flown.

He's perfect. Chubby cheeks, big green eyes like his mother's, and a mop of dark hair like mine. He's got that toddler stubbornness—already independent, wanting to take on the world. And every time I say his name, I'm reminded of the friend who gave his life for us. It's a bittersweet thought, but one that makes me proud.

He wriggles in my arms. "Yeah, I know. You've got things to do," I mutter with a smirk, hoisting him higher onto my hip.

We head downstairs, Sasha still babbling away. "Snack! 'Nana!"

"Coming right up, little man," I say as I place him in his highchair, pulling out his breakfast as he keeps up his toddler chatter.

I cut up a banana and add it to a small bowl of oatmeal, which I set in front of him. He digs in happily, babbling between bites.

"Glad you approve, little man," I say, moving over to the stove to prepare breakfast for Amelia and me.

A few minutes later, she comes down the stairs, looking as amazing as ever in a simple pair of jeans and a T-shirt. How does she manage to make everything look good? She glances around, like she's searching for something.

"What's up?" I ask, catching her eye.

She grins, her eyes lighting up. "We're already into December, and we still haven't put up the Christmas decorations."

I nod. "Say no more. We'll go tree shopping this weekend. Get this place looking festive in no time."

She seems pleased with that, walking over and kissing me on the cheek. "Good answer."

As we sit down for breakfast, she starts talking about work, specifically, the new bakery location she and Claire are planning to open across town. "It's a lot, but I'm excited. This could really take us to the next level."

I smile, proud of her. "You'll crush it. No doubt."

"And what about you?" she asks, raising an eyebrow. "How's work going?"

"Good. I just locked in a few high-paying cybersecurity contracts. They'll keep me busy but still give me plenty of time for you and Sasha. That's my top priority."

Her smile tells me I made the right call.

As we finish breakfast, Amelia gets a text from Claire. She checks it, then glances up at me with a smile. "Claire's asking if we want to do a playdate at Dolores Park in an hour or so."

I'm always down for Sasha and William to hang out. The two of them are becoming fast friends. "Sounds good to me," I say, scooping Sasha out of his highchair. "He could use some outdoor time."

We clean up the kitchen and head out, Sasha bouncing in my arms as we make our way to the car. As we walk, I glance at Amelia. "How's the next book coming along?"

She grins, that familiar spark in her eyes. "It's still in the idea phase. Honestly, I'm still basking in the success of *The Duke's Secret Heir*—it blew up beyond what I expected."

"That's because it's good," I remind her. "But don't let it go to your head," I add with a playful wink.

She laughs, nudging me with her elbow. "Don't worry, I won't. I'm simply happy to let the muse visit whenever she's ready."

I raise an eyebrow. "Like Jack Kerouac said, 'Sometimes you have to chase the muse down.'"

"Chase her down, huh?" she teases, glancing over at me. "Guess I better start running then."

As we make our way to Dolores Park, the clouds start to part, letting some sunshine break through. We round a corner, and suddenly the city stretches out before us, a perfect view of the bay, the skyline, and the people coming and going, living their lives. I pause for a second, taking it all in.

Amelia glances up at me, curiosity filling her eyes. "What's wrong?"

"Nothing," I tell her. "In fact, everything is exactly right."

She tilts her head, still looking confused. "What do you mean?"

I take a deep breath, realizing this is it, the moment I've been waiting for. "There's something I've been wanting to ask you. But there's never been the right time. Until now."

Confusion shadows her face, but I see a flicker of realization starting to form as I reach into my coat pocket. I pull out the small box I've been carrying with me for weeks, and her eyes go wide as she stares at it.

This is it. The life I never thought I could have, right in front of me.

I take a deep breath, locking eyes with her, feeling the weight of the moment settling in. "You came into my life when I least expected it. I wasn't looking for anyone and yet, there you were. You've made me realize that I don't want to live without you. I can't. Not now, not ever."

Her eyes glisten as I continue. "I want to start this next chapter with you and Sasha together, as a family. I can't imagine my life any other way."

I open the box, revealing the ring inside. Her hands fly to her mouth, and I drop to one knee, the words coming easily. "Amelia, will you marry me?"

She gasps, and then the tears spill over. "Yes!" she exclaims. "Yes, yes, a thousand times, yes!"

I slip the ring onto her finger, my heart filled with more joy than I've ever known. I stand back up as she wipes her eyes, grinning at me, her smile radiant. But then she takes my hand, placing it on her belly. I feel the warmth of her skin, and suddenly, it clicks.

I blink, processing what she's trying to say. "You mean—"

She nods, her smile growing even wider. "We're having another baby."

I fist pump the air, excitement rushing through me. Sasha, watching us from his stroller, giggles, sensing the good vibes. I pull her close, our lips meeting in a tender kiss, as we whisper our I love you's.

And just like that, happily ever after begins—again.

The End

Printed in Great Britain
by Amazon